SCRIPT TO SLAY

ST. MARIN'S COZY MYSTERY 6

ACF BOOKENS

1

I sat in my reading chair and looked out the window. The snow had started overnight, and the forecast was for it to continue well into the morning. I was so excited. We almost never got snow out here on Maryland's Eastern Shore, and I loved snow, especially if it snowed me in, which was the case today. All of St. Marin's was basically shut down because, well, because we didn't have a snowplow. The town had never invested in one, and I had to say that seemed wise to me. Now, all of us could just stay in and read with hot cocoa and extra marshmallows.

Many of my neighbors were not of my perspective, though, my mother included. She had texted no fewer than nine times to lament how awful it was that she couldn't get out. After the ninth message, I had replied, "Urgent meeting today? Medications to fill? Friend without food?" Her extended silence followed by the acidic "Hardy har har" in reply told me that she'd gotten my point. My mother was retired, and while she stayed busy with charity events – a volunteer gig that she was incredibly good at – she had no need to go out. She and Dad had enough food to keep the town fed in light of the apoca-

lypse, and they'd put in a whole house generator when they'd
bought their condo. So even if the power went out, they'd be
warm and toasty.

As would I, by my fire with a lap blanket, my chubby cat,
Aslan, and my hound dog, Mayhem. Plus, I wouldn't have
that pesky hum of the generator. My bookstore was closed for
the day, and I was going to enjoy the quiet. Alone. It was
blissful.

My best friend and roommate, Mart, had stayed over at her
boyfriend, Symeon's, house the night before, and my fiancé,
Daniel, was out and about with his tow truck helping people
out of ditches – both those who thought they could drive in
snow but couldn't and those brave souls who had to drive
because of work. He'd be gone all day most likely, so I was
already hunkering down with Angie Thomas's new book,
Concrete Rose, and coffee. I could pretend I'd miss Daniel – and I
would in a mild kind of way that gave me a little pause when I
thought too hard about it – but mostly I was just giddy with the
quiet. The quiet of snow was absolute, and it felt like my spirit
needed that relief.

I HAD JUST MADE it through the first half of Thomas's stellar
book when my phone dinged. I rolled my eyes, expecting Mom
to be whining about how she can't stand to be trapped in her
luxury condo on the water for one more minute, and picked up
my phone. It was Daniel. "Headed down the shore to help with
a multi-car pile-up near the Bay Bridge. Don't think I'll make it
back safely tonight. I'm sorry. Stay warm."

I sighed, let myself ponder the lack of "I love you" in his
message for a minute, and then remembered that he was out
helping people . . . and that this meant I had the entire day to
do with as I wished. "Oh, I'm sure everyone will be so grateful.
Drive safely," I replied in kind with a pang of something I wasn't

willing to consider. Then I tucked the phone under my leg and started reading again.

Sometime around three p.m. and eighteen slices of cheese and a bowl of popcorn later, I unfolded myself from under Aslan, much to her annoyance, and decided to don all the cold weather clothing I owned – scarf, hat with ear flaps, a massive eggplant-purple parka, and my fleece-lined boots to go for a walk. Mayhem would have gladly done her business at the edge of the porch to avoid getting her feet wet, but given the opportunity to pull me bodily through snow banks, she managed to muster up a tail wag as I put on her leash.

Once we were out the door, the bracing cold and the bright light of the newly showing sun told me we'd made the right call. I could feel the blood starting to pick up in my circulatory system just to keep my body warm. So Mayhem and I headed out through the six or so inches of show that my friends in the northern climes would scoff at as "a dusting." Here, though, this was a named Blizzard, Blizzard Paco. I didn't understand this phenomenon of naming every storm, not just hurricanes, but at least I knew how to address the air around me as I walked. "Paco, thanks for this. I appreciate the day off and the beauty. So yeah, thanks," I said out loud as Mayhem and I turned onto the wonderland that was our town's Main Street after a snow storm.

Everything was glittering, and there were tufts of snow on the streetlamps and awnings. Someone with a plow on their pick-up had graciously done one pass up the street, so the piles of snow by the sidewalk were substantial. Up ahead, I could see some of my fellow shopkeepers beginning to shovel their square feet of sidewalk. I sighed and decided to do my duty, too, even though I kind of wanted to simply go on back home, finish Thomas's book, and binge the new season of *Glow Up* that I'd been saving for a special day.

I trudged over to the hardware store and bought their only

remaining snow shovel. It was a massive thing, bright yellow and built like a front-end loader, but it did the trick. Within a few minutes, I had the sidewalk in front of my store clear, and I was making my way across the parking lot between my shop and the garden center. Mayhem had insisted on going into the bookstore, so she was now watching me intently from the warmth of my shop's front window. She had such a hard life.

I was just heading back to stow my new shovel at my shop after digging out a couple more store fronts for friends when I heard my name. I looked up from where'd I'd been trying to pry individual snowflakes from the concrete and saw Max Davies, the man who owned the French restaurant up the street from me, smiling and waving. Well, I think it was what you'd call a wave. Max's hand moved like it was a mechanized part of an early robot, all stiff and awkward. But he was definitely calling me, and soon his stiff waved turned into an awkward beckoning motion.

I shot Mayhem a look and secretly hoped she'd nudge the store door open and make a break for it so I could chase her down in the snow rather than talk to Max, but she just looked back at me, forehead wrinkled, like she was enjoying the strange show. I sighed, propped my shovel against my store door, and walked down to Max.

Max Davies was a nice enough man if you liked arrogant, know-it-alls who think they are God's gift to, well, you in particular. Max had a serious thing for me, and while I always felt awkward saying that when someone asked why he kissed my hand for so long on every greeting, it was the truth, a truth I hated. He'd been pursuing me in his really off-base way ever since I'd moved to town more than a year ago, and despite the fact that Daniel and I were engaged, he hadn't slowed down in his pursuits at all. More than once I'd thought about telling him what he could do with his slobbering hand kisses, but St. Marin's is a small town . . . and I didn't want drama . . . okay, I didn't want conflict. Drama just seemed to be part of Max's way in the world.

Now, he was grinning at me like he'd just seen snow for the first time, and I braced myself. This couldn't be good. "Hi Max. What's up?" I said as I stopped a safe two feet away and kept my hands in my pockets.

"Bonjour, Mademoiselle," he said with his fake French accent. Max was from Baltimore, and while he made the best risotto I'd ever had, there was nothing actually French about him. "I see you have been working hard for hours, and I wanted to invite you in for your favorite to help warm you up."

I looked at my watch. I'd been shoveling for thirty minutes, not exactly hours, but I was cold . . . and if he was talking about his mushroom risotto, he was right. It was my favorite, and I was starving. Still, I hesitated.

The problem was that Max often thought I should like things even when I didn't. One time, he'd brought me a chocolate dessert flavored with orange liqueur after I'd told him specifically that I didn't like chocolate and fruit together. He had made some comment about me just needing help to train my palate, and I had shoved the dessert in front of Mart, who had devoured it with revenge-filled glee. So while I was tempted by the idea of risotto, I couldn't be sure he'd actually give me risotto. Plus, I could be sure he would be there, and that alone was just about enough reason to walk away.

But I was cold and hungry, and a quick scan of the street told me that no one was going to come, not even my dog, to rescue me. So I nodded and trudged along behind him into his restaurant. It was warm inside, and Max had a fire roaring in the fireplace that was the centerpiece of the room. I could hear someone knocking around in the kitchen. For a moment, I wondered if it was Symeon, Mart's boyfriend, but then I remembered that her text earlier had said he'd taken the day and that Max was okay with it because the sous chef was available for the limited fare they'd offer to anyone who stopped by. Anyone being me, it seemed. The rest of the dining room was empty.

Max gestured for me to sit in the front window, and I wondered if he wanted to use me as bait for other customers. But then I realized, with a little surprise, that it was actually the best seat in the house. The raised platform by the window gave me a view up and down Main Street, and I could see the white lights that most shopkeepers left up in their windows year-round reflecting off the snow as dusk began to settle in. The sky was that pearl-gray of a winter's afternoon, and with the slight breeze off the water that was picking up tendrils of snow, it looked like a postcard. I found myself strangely grateful that Max had invited me in.

Even when he showed up with a warm mug of wine without asking me if I'd like any, I couldn't muster up enough snark to comment. Instead, I took the heavy ceramic mug in both hands and took a sip of the sweet white wine that was spicy and lemony, and then I sighed. It was really good. Max then brought me a salad full of spicy arugula and dressed with a vinaigrette that was tangy and rich. Finally, he carried over a beautiful, ceramic bowl full of his mushroom risotto, and I almost groaned out loud. I don't know what he did to make that dish so amazing, but on this evening in this setting, it felt like I was going to be eating ambrosia, the food of the gods.

After Max set down the bowl, I thought he might decide to join me, especially given the quiet in his restaurant, but instead, he smiled and walked away. I was grateful. There was something about this meal in this place by myself that felt sacred, special, and while I knew that I should be missing Daniel, I also knew that some of the most memorable times in my life were when I had chosen to be alone. I had a feeling this would be one of those times.

I savored every morsel of that risotto and had just set down my spoon when Max returned with a slice of apple galette that looked divine. It was caramelized on the bottom, and across the top, Max had drizzled just the lightest bit of cinnamon glaze. As he set the plate in front of me, he said, "I decided ice cream might be too much, but if you'd like some—"

I put up my hand. "No, this is perfect." I looked up at my host and smiled, maybe really smiled at him for the first time. "Thank you, Max. This has been an incredible meal." And I meant it. Somehow, this was exactly what I needed to end this restful, magical day.

I ate my dessert and waited for Max to return so I could ask for my bill. When he came back, he handed me a waiter's notebook, and inside it said, "For Harvey. With my compliments. Thank you for treasuring my food as I treasure you." I stared at the note and smiled. Then I looked up and waved to Max who was standing at the bar with a small smile on his face.

I never would have guessed it, but tonight Max had shown that some woman, someday, would win a fine man's heart. I smiled and bowed my head. Then, I slipped on my coat and hat and headed toward the door.

The sun was almost down, and I took one last deep breath of the warm air before I stepped back into the cold again. Then, I heard Max yell, "Get help, Harvey. Get help!"

Bless my heart, I almost didn't turn around because I assumed this was some ruse on Max's part to get me back in so he could ruin a lovely evening with skeeziness. But something about his tone of voice sounded authentic, so I stepped back inside and looked around. He was nowhere to be seen. "Max?"

"Over here, Harvey. Call 911." His voice was coming from behind the bar.

As I rushed over, I took out my phone and dialed, but as soon as the operator picked up, I realized I didn't know what to tell her. So I jumped up and stretched over the bar so I could see. There, crumpled in a heap, was a young woman. "Is she alive, Max?"

He stared up at me and gave a little shake of his head. "I don't think so."

I realized then that the operator was still on the line and asking me if everything was alright. "Someone's dead," I said, too stunned to be tender with my words. "Send help." I gave her the address and hung up.

Then, I raced around the bar and squeezed in next to Max. Normally, I would be doing my best to avoid this close a quarters with my quasi-stalker, but a good risotto free of come-ons and a dead body will disrupt any person's norms. "You know her, right?"

Max rolled his eyes at me. "Of course, I know her. This is Lizzie, my bartender."

I felt a tiny pang of both annoyance and relief that Max was, it appeared, back to being his condescending self. I crouched down and tried to get a look at the young woman's face, but she was folded over, her face buried in her shins. "Do I know her?"

Max shook his head. "I just hired her last week. Tonight was her first night."

"Killed on her first night at a new job." I was trying to keep my brain from spinning as it began to ask the questions that sprang to mind when I encountered something I didn't understand. My friends called me *nosy,* but I preferred the term *curious.* Still, now was not the time. "Do you know if she had family?"

"I don't normally take a full genealogy when I interview my employees, so no," Max's voice was clipped and hard, but I decided to cut him some slack given the circumstances.

A few seconds later, I could hear a siren making its way up the street more slowly than usual. The snow was impeding even the sheriff's progress, I supposed. Eventually, though, I heard the crunch of tires out front, and then the door of the restaurant opened as Tucker Mason, the sheriff of St. Marin's came in, shaking off his ball cap and stomping his feet. The last few melting snowflakes stood out against his brown skin.

I waved Tuck over, and he sighed when he saw me. I, largely for reasons beyond my own control, I would argue, had ended up involved in the surprising number of murders that cropped up in St. Marin's. At first, I had butted in, trying to help as was my way and finding out that my idea of help was the sheriff's idea of hindrance. Now, I tried to stay out the way, even if my curiosity sometimes got the better of me. "I was here for dinner. That's all," I said defensively as the sheriff reached the bar.

"That's true," Max said. "Neither of us knew Lizzie was back here during the entire meal."

Tuck raised an eyebrow and looked at me. "You two were having dinner?"

I shook my head vigorously. "Um, no. Max made a splendid meal for me because I'd come into town and shoveled snow. We did not, however, dine together." I stared hard at Tuck. He was a good friend, and he knew how much Max's advances annoyed me. Plus, as discreet as he was, I knew that if he suspected anything untoward, he would tell Daniel, and I didn't want Daniel worrying for what was truly no reason.

Tuck smiled. "Got it. Okay, so who is this?" He knelt down by Lizzie's body, double-checked her pulse, and then lifted her head.

"This is Lizzie Bordo, my new bartender," Max said.

I couldn't help myself: I snickered. "Lizzie Bordo . . . your bartender. That's not her real name is it?"

Max furrowed his brow and stood up to look at me. "What do you mean?"

"Come on, Max. You hired a bartender named Lizzie Bordo . . . like the wine." I tilted my head and looked at him out of the corner of my eye.

"Oh, that . . ." He shrugged.

"I was actually thinking Lizzie Borden," Tuck said as he stood. "Seems oddly fitting."

"Because she was axed to death?" I looked again to see if I had missed a copious amount of blood but didn't see a thing.

"Well, no, but just because she's goth and, well, dead." The sheriff came around the bar and sighed. "Sorry, that was disrespectful. It's been a long day, and it now looks," he glanced at the bar, "like it's going to be a long night."

I couldn't even imagine. I knew that Tuck had probably been out helping stranded motorists most of the day, and I knew he wouldn't let Lizzie's death go uninvestigated even until morning.

"Do you know if she had family?" Tuck asked Max.

I snickered again. "Max doesn't take a family genealogy when he does an interview, Tuck, geez."

Max sneered. "I do have an emergency contact if that would be helpful."

Tuck nodded with exaggeration. "I'd say this qualifies as an emergency, Max. Could you get that information, please?"

With a huff, Max went into the back room, and Tuck pulled out a chair at the nearest table. "Did you know her?"

I shook my head as I sat down next to him. I knew this routine. I had to answer a few questions before I could head out. "Didn't even know she was here until Max found her as I was leaving. Any idea how she died?"

"If I did, would I tell you?" The sheriff gave me a pointed look.

"Understood. Poor woman. It was her first night." I looked over at the bar and realized that despite the warmth of my meal and the actual hospitality of Max, my image of a pleasant night was now ruined because a woman had lay dead the whole time just behind the bar. Then, a horrible thought struck me. "Tuck, do you have any idea how long she's been dead?"

He put his hand on mine. "A while, Harvey. A few hours, I'd

say." He squeezed my fingers. "Don't worry. You couldn't have helped her."

I sighed as relief and sadness pulsed under the skin on my throat. "Okay." I let out a long slow breath. "What do you need from me?"

"I think I've got it," Tuck said as he took out his notebook. "Keep this quiet for now, okay, Harvey?"

I nodded. "Right. Wouldn't want the St. Marin's grapevine to reach her family before you do?"

"Precisely."

Alas, even though I kept my mouth shut about Lizzie's death and decided not to even tell Daniel or Mart until the next day, Tuck and I underestimated the power of the scanner-owning community in St. Marin's. By the time Mayhem and I made the walk home, Mart had texted twice and even called once to see if I was okay since the dispatcher's call for police presence had included my name because I'd made the 911 call.

Symeon kept a scanner going at his house because he worked as a volunteer firefighter. I knew this because when, one night, I'd forgotten my keys and called the dispatcher at the sheriff's office to see if Tuck could swing by to help me out since he wasn't answering his cell phone, the request had gone out by radio, a fact that I would never live down. But I also wouldn't ever be locked out because the entire police department and fire department donated to make me twelve sets of keys. I now had them stashed everywhere.

I took off Mayhem's leash and was just dialing Mart's number when I heard a vehicle in the driveway.

I looked out and Daniel's wrecker had parked behind my

car and he and his Basset Hound, Taco, were jogging across the snowy driveway. Daniel looked anxious, so I tugged the door open and shouted, "I'm fine," and waved my phone. Unfortunately, my shout distracted Daniel from watching his footing, and he took a nosedive into the snow-covered azaleas in the front of our house. Taco, with his almost stomach-draggingly-low center of gravity, kept his footing and watched his master tumble.

I rushed out to see if he was okay and slipped on the sidewalk I hadn't bothered to shovel, and a moment later, Mayhem was standing over me as if to say, "Why exactly are you on the ground?" I groaned and rolled over to look at Daniel. He was already on his feet and headed my way. He helped me up, and when he saw I was okay – both from the 911 call that he had also heard and the fall – he began to laugh. I could tell he was trying to suppress it because his shoulders were shaking, but eventually, I got giggling. Soon, we were slipping our way back to the house as we laughed out loud.

Aslan greeted us at the open door and whisked her tail. Clearly, the cold air was annoying her highness because when we got in the house, she headed back to my room, where I was sure she'd taken up her throne on the chenille throw I left at the foot of my bed for just that purpose.

Once we were all settled, dried off, and warming up by the fire Daniel quickly built, he turned to me and said, "So what happened?

I put my hands on either side of his face. "You're not usually a worrier. Long day?"

"Just too many cars in ditches. Too many people hurt because of reckless choices."

I looked outside and saw a few stars coming out. "Looks like the worst is over, though. Looks like your duties are over for the night." I knew I should ask him to stay, but I had kind of been looking forward to having the evening to myself, especially after the shock of finding out a woman had been killed in the place I had dinner.

Daniel kissed my cheek. "Well, since I am my own boss and most of the main roads are now clear, I'm all yours for the evening." He stood up. "But before you tell me about your excitement, any chance you have some leftovers I can heat up? I'm starving."

I smiled. "You sit. I'll fix homemade hamburger helper just for you." I didn't often get a chance to cook, and while this meal wasn't exactly extravagant, it was filling and one of Daniel's favorites. Plus, I could have it ready in twenty minutes.

So while I browned ground beef and slid the macaroni and other ingredients into the largest skillet I owned, I told Daniel about Lizzie's death and caught him up on my dinner at Max's place and his strangely respectful behavior.

"Maybe he's actually going to succeed in wooing you away," Daniel said with a tiny bit of tension in his voice that I decided to ignore.

"Well, he does make a great risotto," I said, pretending to ponder my options. "But he got pretty snarky with me later, so I think you're safe."

"Hey Siri, take a note," Daniel said into the air.

"What do you want your note to say?" the phone in Daniel's pocket responded.

"Learn how to make mushroom risotto," Daniel said.

I laughed.

WE SPENT the rest of the night watching *Outer Banks* and answering texts from our friends as the word about Lizzie's death spread. I talked Daniel into the show on the promise of a treasure hunt, and he put up with my love of teenage drama because he was a good guy. By the time I headed to bed and Daniel took up his spot on the couch, Taco and Mayhem were putting on a full snore symphony by the fire, and everyone knew about the young woman who had died in Max's restaurant. The odd thing was, however, that no one knew her, not even a little, and in a place as small and close as St. Marin's that's rare and cause for a full-on gossip-driven investigation.

By the time I reached All Booked Up the next morning, the gossip train had created a mythic version of Lizzie Bordo that incorporated a tragic past in a mansion outside Baltimore, a deranged ex-boyfriend who was after her millions, and a false identity. I had my doubts about the first two, but I could not imagine that someone had actually named their child Lizzie Bordo, so I thought an alias was pretty likely. Still, I didn't like to speculate about people's lives. Each of us has stories, hard stories usually, and I don't know anyone who wants someone else deciding who gets to know those stories and how. So I decided to wait to hear what Tuck wanted to share when he was ready.

Meanwhile, I kept myself busy putting out the new releases. Tuesday was new book day everywhere, and while I had known what titles were going on sale that day for weeks, I never got over the thrill of sliding a new title onto the shelf. Today, I was particularly jazzed to put out the sequel to Hafsah Faizal's fantasy series and *Remote Control* by Nnedi Okorafor, an author whose work I simply adored. I loved fantasy novels, and people were often surprised by that fact. Something about me – my sort of "boho meets farm-girl" look, my love of dogs, my often wild hair? – made people think I only read literary fiction. I loved literary fiction, but give me magic or some sort of supernatural entity, and I'm all in.

By the time I had the front tables rearranged with Faizal's and Okorafor's books featured, last week's new releases shuffled back just a bit on the displays, and the new orders I'd requested to replace titles we'd just sold, it was almost noon, and I was starving. The English muffins that Daniel and I had toasted with honey and peanut butter that morning had long since worn off, and I was ready for something delicious.

Daniel must have picked up on the strong taco vibes I was sending his way because he appeared just as I was about to text him and say, "Chicken with mole." He was carrying two bags stamped with our friend Lu's logo. Lu ran the best food truck on the Eastern Shore, and she served her family's recipes of classic Mexican fare. Most days, I chose her carnitas tacos, but her mole sauce was calling to me today. Fortunately, the taco vibes were strong, and Daniel had brought just what I wanted.

We were just sitting down to eat in the backroom of the store when I heard the bell ring over the front door and then, a moment later, saw my assistant manager, Marcus's, head pop around the breakroom door. "Tuck and Lu are here," he said. "I assume it's okay to send them back unless you want me to tell the sheriff and the woman whose food you are about to inhale to come back later." He winked.

Marcus was the best assistant manager in the world. He knew books. He loved his job, and while he respected me as his boss, he didn't hesitate to tease me like a friend should. He knew I'd want to see Tuck, and since I adored not only Tuck's wife's food but his wife herself, I was always happy to see them both. "Please, send them back," I said in my most ostentatious voice.

Two seconds later, the couple burst through the door with their arms spread and said, in unison, "We have arrived," as if they had just come to a great ball at some fine castle.

"We come bearing gifts," Tuck said with a bow as he held out two plates of dulce de leche cake.

I grinned. "Well, then, fine people, you are welcome."

Daniel stood, bowed slightly, and pulled out two chairs. When our friends had stepped in front of their chairs, he slid Lu's chair into the back of her knees, and she sat down with a dainty lilt of her hands. When Daniel moved toward Tuck's seat, the sheriff raised a hand and said, "Thanks. I've got this."

For a few moments, we all ate in silence. Apparently, Daniel had known they were coming because there were enough tacos for all of us. Well, there were enough for all of us if I didn't eat four. But I showed restraint.

When we'd all had our fill of mole and cake, I looked at Tuck expectantly and said, "I so appreciate the cake, but you know the gift I desire most."

Tuck rolled his eyes but then grinned mischievously. "What makes you think I have information to share?"

It was my turn to roll my eyes. "Seriously, the only time you come in this store is when you have an investigation under way. If I didn't know you have a deep affinity for Wallace Stegner and William Least Heat Moon, I'd think you a disparager of books."

Tuck sighed. "You forgot to add A. S. Byatt to your list of my favorites."

I laughed. Tuck was one of the few men and the only black man I personally knew who appreciated the British author as much as I did. He and I had bored Lu and Daniel almost to death one night at dinner when we'd starting discussing her book *Babel Tower,* and about once a week, we made some obscure Byatt reference that only we get. It was amazing.

But he wasn't much of a book buyer. Unlike me, he re-read his favorites over and over. I however almost never re-read because of my ever-increasing conviction that I would die before I read everything I wanted to read. Tuck went deep; I went wide. It was a classic clash of reading styles, but I didn't mind. Any person who read anything with passion was good in my book.

"So, what's the news?" I asked with boldness.

The sheriff scowled at me briefly and then said, "Lizzie was murdered. Strangled, I think. But that's just information. I actually need your help."

I sucked in a quick breath. Most of the time Tuck wanted me to butt out of his investigations, and for good reason. So the fact that he needed my help wasn't just exciting, it was rare, the best kind of exciting. "Of course. What can I do?"

Next to me, Daniel shifted in his seat and moaned quietly. He really, really hated my curiosity. Really hated it.

He sighed. "Well, we were right about Lizzie's name. There's no mention of a woman fitting her description and named Lizzie Bordo that goes back more than six months. It's like she appeared out of thin air."

I nodded. "So it was an alias. I hoped so. Otherwise, she had either intensely cool or profoundly cruel parents." I sat back and let my mind leap around for a few seconds. A woman who applied for a job as a bartender chose a misspelling of a wine for her name but also chose a name that referred back to a famous ax murderer. "She chose that name for a very specific reason," I blurted as the realization hit me.

Tuck nodded. "That's what I'm thinking, too, which is why I need your help." He looked down at his hands, and I saw a flush rush over his cheeks.

I squinted at my friend. He wasn't telling me something. "Okay, tell me why you need my help, and tell me what I'm not going to like about what you're going to say."

The sheriff's eyes flashed up to mine, and he shrugged. "Good news or bad news?"

"Bad news. Always bad news first. Leaves me with something to look forward to."

"Okay, I need you to work with Max." He leaned back as if he thought I might smack him, and I might have if I wasn't opposed to even minor – and well-deserved – acts of violence.

"Why?" I spat the word. Even the generous and thoughtful meal last night could not make up for Max's ham-handed courting of me, especially not after his snarky attitude when we found Lizzie's body.

"Max is a sommelier," Tuck said.

I groaned. "So he's going to investigate the Bordeaux angle, and I'm supposed to take on the Lizzie Borden one, right?"

Tuck looked at Daniel. "She's a smart one."

"She's not that smart if she agrees to this escapade," Daniel replied as he gave me a long, significant look of warning. "Just say no, Harvey."

I stared at Daniel, looked back at Tuck, smiled at Lu, and then shoved most of a taco in my mouth to buy some time before answering. Despite the fact that Tuck had been the first to remark on the victim's name and the reference to one of the most infamous murderers in American history, I was actually the Lizzie Borden aficionado. My interest in her came in college when a postmodern fiction professor who let us call him by his first name and was, thus, immediately the best professor in the world, introduced me to the work of Angela Carter.

Carter's feminist retellings of fairy tales – like when Beauty actually liberates herself from the Beast instead of staying to love him despite of his imprisonment of her – sparked something in me that spoke of truth. Don't get me wrong. I love a dancing tea cup and grandfather clock as much as anyone, but I needed, especially as I entered adulthood, to see a woman challenge much of what was accepted about how women should be treated. Carter was my entrance into a world where women were powerful equals who took control of their own fates. I fell in love with her work immediately.

Then, when I read her take on Lizzie Borden's actions in her story "The Fall River Axe Murders," I became a fan for life. Carter's story suggested that Lizzie had PMDD and had perhaps been a victim of abuse within her family. Thus, her alleged actions were, perhaps, justified. I didn't know if I agreed with the idea that anything justified the brutal murder of anyone, but the story led me down a life-long fascination with Lizzie Borden. I'd read everything I could about her, about the murders, and about what was clearly an incomplete investigation and too-quick arrest of the young woman. To say I was a Lizzie Borden encyclopedia would not be overstating.

All that's to say, I knew why Tuck was asking for my help – if this young woman had taken a name to reference Lizzie Borden, I was the one who could figure out why. I had made my fascination with her known my first October in town when I'd dressed as her for Halloween, ax and all.

I swallowed the last morsels of delicious taco and then nodded. "Okay, I'll help, but only on two conditions: first, I am not talking with Max. If he and I need to share information we do it through email with you copied in. I want a witness to any of his nonsense."

Daniel sighed. He wasn't happy, but he wasn't protesting much. And I knew he'd like that email provision. I also knew he'd really like my next condition.

"Secondly, no one outside of this room can know I'm helping. I don't want to get involved in any other aspect of the investigation. I don't want to talk to anyone but the three of you about this. Agreed?"

Tuck looked at Daniel and then at Lu, and then as if on cue, all three of them started to laugh. Then, they started to guffaw. Within seconds, tears were streaming out of Daniel's eyes.

I stared at my friends and felt anger rising in my chest. "What is so funny?" I shouted.

None of them could stop laughing long enough to explain, but Daniel kept trying and then having to hold up a finger while he collapsed into laughter again.

Finally, they began to get control of themselves, and Daniel took my hand. "Harvey, dear Harvey, your condition is reasonable except for one thing."

I was bewildered. "What?!"

"You," Lu and Tuck said at the same moment.

I stared at my friends, expecting one of them to explain, but they just looked at me as they tried to keep bubbles of laughter to keep from bursting from their mouths. "What are you talking about? I don't understand."

Daniel, all mirth gone from his eyes now that he could see I was really confused, caught his breath and said, "Harvey, I'm sorry. It feels so obvious to us, but apparently, it's not to you." He squeezed my fingers and said gently but directly. "Love, you cannot keep a secret to save your life."

"Literally," Tuck added with a gentle smile. "I won't tell anyone a thing, and I'm sure Lu and Daniel are happy to do the same. But Harvey, if you really don't want anyone to know what you're doing for this investigation, it's you that needs telling to be quiet."

I scowled at my friends and wanted to storm out in self-righteous anger. But somewhere behind my ribs, I knew they were right. I hated secrets and was, thus, terrible at keeping them. Privacy I respected – I didn't gossip, and I didn't share stories that weren't mine to tell – but secrets usually came with dark underbellies, and I loathed the way they often infected the people who kept them. In the past, I'd been entrusted with some big secrets, secrets related to murder, and I had not even once kept one of those secrets. I didn't regret that, but I could see what my friends were saying.

I dropped my head back over the top of my chair and looked at the ceiling. Then, I slowly lifted my head and said, "You're right."

Daniel kissed the tips of my fingers. "So do you want to withdraw that second condition?"

I shook my head. "No, I want to modify it. No one but our people can know. But I want all of us to know. We're having a picnic in the store tonight."

Lu stood and helped Tuck to his feet. "I'm bringing hot toddies," she said.

"I like this plan, " Tuck said with a kiss on his wife's cheek. "Seven? I'll ask Cate to coordinate food."

I nodded. "Good. I'll gather some preliminary information, connect with Max," I felt my chest constrict at the very thought, "and be ready to share tonight."

"Cool," Tuck said as he opened the break room door before quickly closing it again. "I almost forgot one thing, and before I tell you, I'm not suggesting this has anything to do with her pseudonym. Not at all."

I raised my eyebrows in query.

He sighed and said, "Lizzie only had one arm."

3

Daniel and I stayed in the break room for a few more minutes, cleaning up the trash from lunch and talking over that bit of information that Tuck had just shared.

"I wish it didn't seem like such a big deal that she was an amputee," I said as I ran a cleaning wipe over the table. "But I'm not that enlightened, I guess. Plus, how did I not notice?"

"Well, Tuck said her missing arm was on the side away from you and she was slumped over. We expect what we consider "normal," I guess, and since you expect most people to have two arms, you didn't notice that she only had one." Daniel's voice was soft, but I could hear the strain in it.

I pursed my lips. "Ugh, I hate that. That's some prejudiced nonsense there in my head. You're right, of course, but how did I ever come to think of "like me" as normal?"

Daniel sighed and squeezed my arm. "But now we know what we think and what's wrong with it, so we can change it. And you get the chance to help bring justice to this woman. That's a good thing in all ways."

I sighed. I knew he was right, but I hated the icky, twisty

feeling in my gut when I realized that I had absorbed some hateful thinking along the ways of life. I didn't want that thinking to stay, of course, but it also meant I was going to have to be uncomfortable a while as I unlearned and retrained my brain. Still, I'd done that unlearning a lot in my life, and I could do it again now.

Daniel and I headed back out on the floor, and he gave Taco a scratch before heading back to his shop. Taco didn't even give his owner a second glance before collapsing prone next to Mayhem in the front window. I kind of wanted to join them in that sunbeam . . . to lay there and nap and think, but I had some reading to do.

But first, time to get the invites out to folks for our store picnic. I texted everyone – Stephen and Walter, my friends from San Francisco who had moved here shortly after Mart and I did; my parents, another couple who wound up in St. Marin's to be close to me; Henri and Bear; Pickle; Woody; Elle; and finally Cate and Lucas. I knew that Tuck would have already talked with Cate, but I had a special request. To the message I had copied and pasted from my previous ones, I added, "Red Velvet with cream cheese frosting."

Almost immediately, a cupcake icon appeared on my screen, and I grinned. With dessert handled, it was time for me to get to work on my research presentation. "Marcus, do we have any books on Lizzie Borden?" I was pretty sure we didn't, but Marcus now kept a tighter eye on our inventory that I did.

"Not that I know of. Oh, wait, there is that Angela Carter story in her collection." He smiled. "Want me to pull it?"

I smiled. "Nope. I know the story, almost by heart. Thanks, though. Maybe, let's do a new window display – "Infamous Women" and put *Burning Your Boats* in there."

"Ooh, so we're doing a 'women who did horrible things' window?" Marcus waggled his eyebrows at his own intentionally obtuse remark.

"Exactly. Let's put misogyny on display, shall we?" I shook my head. "So Lizzie Borden, Amelia Earhart, Joan of Arc, Ruby Bridges, Fannie Lou Hamer, Malala. . . you get the picture."

"Totally. I'm on it." He headed toward the cafe and his girl-friend, Rocky. "Want to help me put women on display?" he said with a wink at me over his shoulder.

"We're doing a porn window?" Rocky quipped.

I loved those two, mostly because I knew they were going to do an amazing tribute to women, despite their witty banter to the contrary. And now, since the store was pretty quiet, I could do some reading for tonight.

TWO HOURS LATER, the window display was up, and it looked amazing. Rocky had cut an airplane out of a discarded box and sketched it out to make it look like Earhart's plane. Then, she'd used her beautiful handwriting to write "Not So Well-Behaved" across the side of the plane. It was perfect, and I decided when I saw it that we'd be keeping this display up through Women's History month in March. We were going to celebrate women for a full eight weeks, and it was going to be glorious.

While Rocky and Marcus had pulled and arranged books, I'd read everything I could find online about Lizzie Borden. She was unmarried. She never left Fall River, even when the community ostracized her after the trial. She never made a public statement about the murders, her arrest, or anything else that I could find. She was famous for something she wasn't believed to have done. It was profoundly ironic, and yet, it felt very 21st century. I wondered if Lizzie Borden would have been a reality star if she lived now.

When I reached the end of the things I could refresh in my mind about Lizzie Borden, I realized I finally had to reach out to Max and hear what he was thinking in terms of the wine angle. I opened my email and entered his address, which I had culled from his website, never having cause or desire to use it before. I told him that I hadn't uncovered anything much that seemed relevant to the murder or his late bartender and Lizzie Borden, and I hoped he was having more success. I stalled out in my note when I got to the sign off. I thought about a typical "Thanks" but could hear Max snarking, "Thanks for what" in the back of my head. "Sincerely" sounded far too formal, and "Best" too stuffy. I went with a simple, "Harvey" and hit send.

Then, I closed my computer and stretched. I'd been hunched over far too long, and I half-expected my spine to crack like popcorn when I straightened it. But without the satisfaction of a string of cracks, I felt disappointed and still achy. I decided my best course of action was to do some heavy lifting to get my blood flowing.

So I headed to the back room and loaded up a library cart so I could fill the overstock shelves in the store with our backstock. We'd had everything full to the brim at the holidays, but in the post-seasonal lull, we'd gotten a bit lax about keeping those spaces looking rich with good reading.

I pushed the cart over to the shelves above the fiction section, stacked books from the crook of my arm to my chin, and hiked myself up the ladder with my other arm. I'd done this a thousand times, but this time, I paid careful attention to the way having both my arms on my body made this easier and required less effort. If I only had one arm, like Lizzie, I'd have had to make more trips and would have been far more tired.

Yet she had been a competent – probably expert bartender given that Max didn't hire anyone who was less than amazing to work in his restaurant. His chef, Symeon, Mart's boyfriend, could have had his pick of Baltimore's or DC's finest restaurants when he began to search for a new job, but the quaintness of St. Marin's had drawn him in, he said. He'd had family here, and once he'd visited, he decided to stay. It was a common story.

Like Three Pines in Louise Penny's books, St. Marin's seemed to draw people to herself and keep them close.

Maybe that's why Lizzie Bordo had come here, to find a quiet place to land. And to use her bartending skills, I presumed. I kept thinking about how I couldn't make a martini with two hands.

I went back to my computer and googled "one-armed bartender." A small part of me thought I might find a video of Lizzie herself, but no such luck. Instead, I watched clip after clip of people with one arm or one hand pouring drinks expertly, and once again, I had to sit with the discomfort that I had presumed a great deal about what someone without a limb could do.

I realized then that I needed to call my mom. I needed her help again. I needed to do something to help myself learn and to just simply help, and I needed Mom to guide me. "Mom, can you come early tonight? I want to talk to you about an event."

"An event?" Mom said. "Now you're talking. Five thirty work?"

"See you then." I hung up and took a deep breath. I need to prepare.

If life on the Eastern Shore was like life in the fictionalized version of the Outer Banks that the Netflix show described, then my mother would be a Kook, a total society lady dedicated to her charities and good works. She'd been organizing volunteer events for years, but she'd come into her full event-planning element here in St. Marin's. Every week she was spearheading or pretending to serve on a committee while actually overseeing a different charity event, and she was really good at it. Every event she'd planned had exceeded its fundraising goal by far.

Thus, I knew I needed to be prepared for our conversation or I, too, would be "coached" right out of my own idea and find my mother coordinating some event that would require me to buy another fancy dress. I needed to have a plan, and a good one. So I opened my computer again and got to work researching organizations that could educate me – and other "abled" people, those of us without disabilities – about the difficulties of operating fully in our society as a person with a disability. I read pages and pages about disability rights, and with each thing I read, I realized I needed to learn a lot more to actually be a supporter of people with disabilities. Moreover, I realized we needed to make some changes in the store.

I read and read and made pages and pages of notes, and by the time five thirty rolled around, I was ready. We were going to hold a fundraiser for the National Disability Rights Network. I had thought about holding it in honor of Lizzie, but since I didn't know the woman, didn't know if she'd want such a thing done for her, and had just learned how humiliating and objectifying it is for events to be held for people with disabilities without having those people present, I decided against it. Instead, I was going to make sure Mom and I organized an event that focused on Disability Rights by having a disabled speaker who would also work with us in every other capacity we could find to make this event inclusive and representative of what true advocacy looked like.

Fortunately, while Mom was terrible at taking direction on event planning itself, she was really open-minded and very aware of when she needed help. So I knew I could ask her to contact the Network and get their guidance on how to appropriately host an event as a fundraiser for them. And when we hunkered down with our planners and two of Rocky's snowflake-decorated decaf lattes, Mom was on board immediately.

"You know, I don't know much at all about disability rights. Is it terrible to say that I haven't ever thought about it before?" She grimaced.

"I think it is terrible, but you're not alone. I hadn't either." I sighed. "It's too bad it took a woman's death for me to be aware." Mom made a note in her planner. "I'm making a call to the Network my top priority for tomorrow. I don't want to set anything in stone until I talk with them, but let's spitball some ideas to share."

I almost spit my latte on my mother. "Since when is "spitball" a term you use?"

"I'm updating my slang to relate to younger people," she said.

I rolled my eyes. "I think you may need to talk with some actually younger people, Mom. I don't think teenagers say 'spitball.' Not even sure they'd know what the original term meant."

"Really?" Mom said with a shrug. "Oh well. I tried." She picked up her phone and began showing me possible locations and themes for our event, and an hour later, we had two good, solid suggestions for fundraising events that would be accessible and fun. I was getting excited.

Since Marcus had handled the evening without me, I sent him out at six thirty and closed up the store by myself. It was a quiet night. The roads were clear, and most of the snow had melted. But Eastern Shore folks didn't contend with snow much, and it had kept most people at home all day. It wasn't going to take me long to reshelve and cash out the register. Besides, I wanted a little quiet time to think about Lizzie and her pseudonym. I couldn't get my mind around why someone would choose a woman accused of murder as her namesake. Did she admire Lizzie? Think she'd been falsely accused?

Or was it more personal? Tuck had said our Lizzie was in her early thirties, like Lizzie Borden. Our Lizzie hadn't worn a ring or said anything, according to Max, that indicated she was married. So maybe the two Lizzies had an affinity as women who were unmarried for longer than most people thought acceptable?

I kept letting my questions flip around in my mind as I tidied the store. I wasn't getting any definitive answers, but I hoped that when Tuck finally figured out Lizzie's given name, we might be able to start pulling threads together.

A bit before seven, I checked my email for the last time and saw a message from Max. Mostly, it was a long sermon on the history of Bordeaux, both the region and the wine, and I almost closed my email before finishing the long message. But his last sentence caught my attention. "Lizzie did tell me that she wished to visit France one day, that she was hoping to settle there, to get away, to start over. Maybe she was going to Bordeaux?"

As someone who had started over not that long ago, Lizzie's statement about that desire rang bells for me. People who were happy didn't pick up their lives and start over. People who were happy didn't do that and also change their names. I had no idea what this woman had gone through in her life, but I felt a connection to her now, as a woman who needed to find a new place in the world. Something was telling me that this wasn't simply about getting a new job or a new haircut. No, such a drastic change of locale and identity signaled something serious. Something scary.

AT SEVEN ON THE NOSE, the bell over the shop door began to ring, and one by one or two by two my friends came into the shop. Mom had run home to pick up Dad and Benji, their dog, and when the three of them arrived, they came with smoked gouda and crackers, which Dad quickly laid out on the counter by the register so people could snack as they came in.

Soon after, Lu and Tuck arrived with her hot toddy makings – a big thermos of decaf coffee and a bottle of whisky. Then came Elle with tulips from her hothouse to set on the table by all the food as well as her weekly delivery of small bouquets for the cafe tables. As Woody helped her set the flowers out, Mart and Symeon arrived with crab dip, a Symeon specialty that almost made me want to like seafood. Almost.

Then, Stephen and Walter carried in a huge bowl of salad made from greens Elle had grown, local goat cheese, and dried cranberries as well as three huge casserole dishes full of Shepherd's Pie. My mouth started watering at just the sight of the browned mashed potatoes. Then, Henri, Bear, and Pickle arrived, and the brownies they carried in – one plate with nuts and one without – scented the shop with chocolate. Cate and Lucas arrived with two platters of red velvet cupcakes from Lucas's side business as a cupcake baker. Finally, Marcus and Rocky joined us, having run out to pick up limeades from a little roadside stand just down Route 13. It was, as always, a veritable feast, and I found myself grateful I'd not snacked all afternoon, even though Rocky's Rice Krispies treats had been tempting me for hours.

Everyone took a sturdy paper plate from the stash I now kept at the store at all times, and soon, we were all quietly filling our faces in chairs and on the floor around the fiction section, our usual gathering place. We'd begun having meals here not long after I'd opened the store, and I loved that the tradition kept going, even if I hated the reason we'd gathered tonight.

Tuck, out of uniform and off-duty, stretched out his legs and said, "Okay, so I know you've heard we had murder yesterday."

"No secret lives long in St. Marin's, Sheriff," Woody said with a smile. "But we don't know much. Is that why we're here?"

Tuck took a sip of his toddy and said, "Well, yes, but first, I need to tell you the very specific reason you're here." He grinned at me and said, "It's because Harvey can't keep a secret."

Every single person in *my* bookstore gasped in mock shock at this not-so-revelatory statement. I sighed. Guess *that* secret was out. Still, it felt good to be known so well by such great people, even if they were taking joy in one of my foibles. "Yes, that's right, friends. I invited you all here to tell you what I would eventually tell you individually by the week's end. I'm helping Tuck with this investigation."

Now, the mock surprise turned to genuine concern because I didn't have the best track record of helping Tuck without getting into some trouble myself. I hurried to explain and calm my friends' fears. "Let me explain. As some of you know, I have a deep interest in Lizzie Borden." I told them about our victim Lizzie's name and the possible tie to the infamous woman of Fall River, Massachusetts.

"Which brings me to something Harvey does not yet know." The sheriff added.

I spun to look at him with fake surprise and said, "What?!"

He smirked and said, "*Our* Lizzie is also from Mass-achusetts. Boston to be exact. And her real name was Cassandra. Cassandra Leicht. She was thirty-four, and so far, we haven't found any record of her being married or having children."

My heart picked up its pace a bit as I realized I may have been on to something with the idea that our Lizzie chose her name because the other Lizzie was also single and childless.

Tuck filled the group in on what we did know – the possible cause of death, Lizzie's amputated arm, and her recent move to St. Marin's to work as a bartender for Max.

"Anything about her parents?" Henri asked.

"Nothing yet, although we know she was born in a hospital, and I found mention of her at a private girls' high school. So it's probably safe to say she came from at least an upper middle class family," Tuck answered.

Well, that was different from Lizzie Borden, I thought. The Bordens hadn't been poverty-stricken, but they definitely weren't wealthy enough to send their daughters to private school.

"Also, I found this in a newspaper article about an elite bartending competition. Our Lizzie won, and they took her picture." He passed around a printed image.

"She's gorgeous," Cate said. "Was she a model?"

When the picture reached me, I saw why Cate had asked. Cassandra, our Lizzie, had the kind of silky brown hair, white porcelain-like skin, and build that was the staid standard of the beauty industry. I could almost picture her on *Next in Fashion*, listening to Tan France critique the clothes she was wearing. "Was she?" I echoed Cate's question

Tuck wrote something in his ever-present notebook, then shook his head. "I didn't find mention of that, but I didn't find much about her at all. Not in a suspicious way. She has social media profiles and a driver's license and such. But most of that stuff was pretty empty." He paused and ran a finger over his shaved head. "It feels a little like she was trying to not be seen or noticed."

"Hard not to be noticed when you look like this," Elle said, holding up the picture. "There's a lot of pressure on women to look a certain way, and while I've never looked the way I was supposed to, I always thought it might be hard to actually fit the standard of beauty, too, like you then had to be what the standard expected."

Something about what Tuck surmised and Elle suggested set off tiny bells in my head, and I asked to see the picture again. Elle passed it over, and I studied the image again. "She has both her arms here." I said it quietly, but the observation was so fundamental, even to me, that everyone heard it.

Tuck held out his hand, and I put the photo in it. He looked at it quickly and said, "Good night. I hadn't even noticed. Thank you, Harvey."

"When was the photo taken?" Bear asked.

"About five years ago," The sheriff said as he scribbled another note.

"Well, that means she's still in recovery from her limb loss." Bear was a doctor, so he would know. "It would take at least a year, probably more, to recover just from the surgery to remove the limb, if there was no injury that required the surgery. If there was and that injury was serious, it would take far longer. But then to be able to work as a bartender again with one less hand, that would have required a lot of focus and practice to be proficient."

Just then, the bell over the door rang, and Max Davies strode in like he had been invited, which he had most certainly not. "Max, what are you doing here?" I shot Tuck a look, and he shrugged. Clearly, no one had expected Max.

"I'm sorry to crash your, er, party, Harvey, but I saw the lights were still on, and I knew you'd want to hear this." He held up a piece of paper, cleared his throat like he about to give his acceptance speech for an Oscar and read, "I, Lizzie Bordo, nee Cassandra Leicht, being of sound mind and body do . . ."

"Whoa, Max," Tuck shot to his feet and took the thin stack of papers out of Max's hands. "This is a legal document, and it needs to be vetted before we share it."

Max, to his small credit, looked a little chagrinned. "You're right. I'm sorry. I just knew it was relevant and wanted Harvey to know. But you're right." He gave a small smile and looked at everyone in the room.

Daniel, kind soul that he was, offered Max a chair, and Max quietly took it with a small thanks.

"Tuck," I said, "since we knew that she left a will, it's okay to talk about that, right? I mean we're not going to know what she left to whom, but it seems significant that a woman as young as she is with no partner or children that we know of made a will, right?"

Tuck sighed. "It does. Max, where did you find this?"

"It was tucked at the back of the cash drawer of our register. I wouldn't have found it normally, but the drawer stuck tonight.

So I took it out to see what had happened, and I found an envelope with that in it behind the drawer."

"Anything written on the envelope?" Tuck asked.

"Not a thing. I thought maybe there were old gift cards or something. I opened it without thinking. Sorry about that, too." Max seemed flustered and off-center, and for the second time in a week, I found myself feeling kindness toward him.

"You okay?" Henri asked him, and I was grateful. I was feeling kind, but I wasn't really interested in opening a heart-to-heart with the man, not just yet.

Max looked up at the ceiling and let out a long breath. "Yes. I am. I didn't think I was that bothered by having Lizzie die. I barely knew her, but, well . . ." His voice trailed off.

Lucas stood up, got Max a red velvet cupcake, and carried it over. "Death is always hard. Murder is harder. And I imagine murder in your place of business is especially hard." He looked at me as he returned to his seat.

He was right. Death in your business felt personal somehow. "Tell us what you did know about her?" I asked.

Max smiled at me, and for the first time, I had the sense that all the swagger and cockiness was a front for a shy person who, if the number of times I'd seen him with other people was any indication, was probably pretty lonely. "She was the best bartender I'd ever seen. And I don't mean with those trick pours and things, although she could do those, too. No, it was more about how she attended to the customers, guided them to a drink they'd like or gave them the perfect version of what they'd asked for. She listened to them, too."

"You saw all that on her first night?" Pickle asked.

Max laughed. "I saw it then, too, but for her interview, I had her work two hours at the bar, and she was amazing." Max looked down at his hands.

"She really was," Symeon added, and I suddenly realized that he had met Lizzie, too. Mart and I hadn't had a chance to talk alone or she probably would have pointed that out. "We have this one older man who comes in every Saturday night and sits alone at the bar. He nurses a gin and tonic every night. Never orders food and only that one drink. He never talks to anyone, but the night Lizzie worked as part of her interview, he talked to her all night. She kept going back to his end of the bar after serving her other customers, and she looked like she was genuinely enjoying their conversation. She was amazing period. But add to that the fact that she was handicapped?"

I winced. All my reading had told me the word *handicapped* was pretty offensive to most disabled people. I wanted to say something, but I didn't. I didn't like that I didn't, but I didn't.

4

The next morning while I ate breakfast, I was still mulling over Max's strange but pleasant change in temperament and pondering Lizzie's skill as a bartender when I felt that niggling in the back of my mind that told me my brain was working on an idea that it wasn't ready to tell all of me yet. That feeling also meant I probably needed to shift my focus to something else and let the back of my mind put in the effort. Fortunately, it was time for me to get to work, and Mayhem and I had a slippery slide-y walk in that was going to take all my concentration.

The hound girl and I made it safely over the patches of black ice, and I was just in time to get the store open and ready. I did a tiny bit of straightening, then flipped on the lights and unlocked the door. To my delight, there, on the other side of the front door glass was Galen, my favorite customer, and he'd brought a friend, a double delight since Galen usually only stopped in on Tuesdays. Already, the day was looking up from the bleak prospects of another below-freezing day on the Eastern Shore that my mind had conjured.

I loved when Galen visited because he knew books and

loved them, first and foremost, but he also always bought books. *And* he highlighted my shop on his very popular Bookstagram feed every time he visited. His Insta game was so strong that he had forced me to up my own and bring in Marcus and Rocky for help in posting daily to our feed and stories. We were up to a few thousand followers, which felt amazing, and I knew I had Galen to thank.

He and his Bulldog, Mack, made their way into the shop while his friend, a tall, thin, Asian woman trailed behind. Unlike many white men in their sixties, my father included, Galen had a wonderfully diverse group of friends, and he often brought them to the store to shop and look around. Today, his guest gravitated right toward the memoir section, and I felt an affinity for her immediately. Memoirs were my go-to when I needed to understand more about how other people experience the world.

While Galen and Mack made their way to the mystery section, where I'd just added a Bulldog-sized bed for his royal highness since he and his owner favored that section above all others, I strolled over and introduced myself to Galen's guest. "Hi, I'm Harvey. So glad you're here. Are you a fan of memoir?"

The woman turned to me and smiled before putting out her hand. "I'm Effie. And yes. I know some people are burnt out on the genre, but not me. I can't get enough. Any you'd recommend?"

Ah, my favorite question in the world. "Well, yes, I do in fact." I winked at my new comrade and said, "This isn't everyone's cup of tea, but this farm memoir, *The Dirty Life,* is splendid. And of course, *The Glass Castle* by Jeannette Walls is a classic."

"You know, I've been wanting to read that one, but it felt too dark, too hard, maybe," Effie said as she picked up the book. "What do you think?"

"It's definitely not a light read, but there's this way Walls handles the trauma of her life that feels uplifting, revelatory, maybe even redemptive." I blushed. "But I don't want to oversell it."

"No worries there. I'm going to dive in. Now, something lighter, too?" she said with a twinkle in her eye. "Maybe something that makes me laugh?"

I didn't hesitate and grabbed David Sedaris's *Calypso* off the shelf and handed it to her. "Just don't read it in public. It's embarrassing to laugh that hard in front of strangers."

"So noted. Thank you." She tucked both books under her arms and turned back to the shelves in the universal book shopper's signal for "I've got it from here."

"Let me know if you need anything," I said and headed off to find Galen.

"Find" was a loose term, though, because in my small shop, the mystery section was just behind the memoir section. So when I rounded the corner, there he was, a stack of titles piled at his feet. "How in the world do you read all these books so quickly?" I said as I eyed his choices. All good ones including *Black Magic Kitten*, a fun cozy with a delightful and magical cat.

"Well, it helps that I'm retired and don't, say, have to run a business." He winked at me. "But I also read really fast."

I squinted at him and said, "Are you a skimmer, Galen?"

"No, ma'am. I read every word, or most every word. Does anyone really read all those 'she saids'? I don't skim. I just read fast." He reached over and patted my arm. "I try not to judge people's reading choices, but I definitely judge people who call skimming reading."

I laughed. "Me, too. Well, I'll be right over there, but of course, you won't need me."

He smiled and turned back to the shelf while I gave the snoring Mack a scratch behind the ears before I went to the counter. Surprisingly, we already had a few customers, most in for coffee from Rocky's cafe, but a few book browsers, too. Maybe the cold wouldn't keep people away after all.

I had just finished up my new book order when Galen and Effie laid their choices on the register. I saw that Effie had added Jenna Wonginrich's *Chicken Scratch* to her pile and smiled. "Going all in on the farm memoir?"

"I figured I might as well. We don't have a lot of farm life in Boston, and while in the boondocks, might as well read about them." Her eyes darted up to mine. "No offense."

"None taken. I'm a proud proponent of the boondocks, at least for me. But glad you're visiting." I smiled, even as I felt the tiny hairs on the back of my neck stand up. Boston.

"Yeah, Effie just showed up on my doorstep last night, a spur of the moment trip." He grinned over at his friend. "Her dad and I were old friends, and I haven't seen you since, well, since you were what, eight or so?"

Effie shrugged. "Something like that. Dad had always talked about this quaint town that you called home, and well, I really wanted to be with someone who knew him on the anniversary." Her voice grew watery and soft. "My dad died five years ago this week," she said quietly.

Galen squeezed her arm. "I'm getting all of these, Harvey. Ring me up."

Effie tried to protest, to get out her own wallet and pay, but Galen was having none of it. I stood there watching them politely bicker over who was paying and wondered if this was how wait staff felt every time diners did this at their tables. If so, I was making it a point to decide who was covering the bill before I ate anywhere again. This was some kind of awkward.

Eventually, Effie graciously conceded, and Galen bought all fifteen books on the stack. I noticed he was trying out Adriana Licio's Basset Hound series and told him that I hoped Mack wouldn't be offended. "We'll just tell him it's a Bulldog." He leaned over the counter and said in a loud whisper. "He's cute but not that bright."

I laughed and tucked the books into the reusable totes Galen always brought on his trips. "How long will you be here?" I asked Effie as I worked the last few titles into the crevices of the bags.

"I'm not sure, actually. I work for myself and brought my cat, so I don't have any reason to be back. I may just hang out a while."

I smiled and ignored the way that niggling query was growing louder in the back of my mind. "Did you tell Mack your cat was a Bulldog, too?"

"No, a ferret," Galen said. "He loves ferrets."

My laughter followed them out the door, and I watched them walk up the street. Effie seemed like a lovely person, but it felt like a very strange coincidence that she ended up in our town just two days after a woman about her age from Boston was killed.

I took out my phone to text Tuck the new information but was interrupted when a young, disheveled man burst into the shop and sent the bell over the door clanging so hard I thought it might fall off.

"Is Max here?" the young man asked as he wheeled up to my counter and stared at me.

It took me a minute to respond because his entrance was so big and his question so odd, but eventually I spit out, "No. Why would Max be here?"

"I saw him here last night during your party or whatever. I thought he might work here or something." A flush of color was moving over the young man's pinkish complexion, and I felt the bluster of his entrance fading away. "He was just here for your party, wasn't he?"

I nodded. "Max owns the restaurant up the street. He was just here with some other," I swallowed hard, "friends. I glanced at the clock on the wall by the door. Eleven fifteen. "He's probably already there if you need him."

The man spun his wheelchair around once, taking in the store, before returning his gaze to me. "I'm sorry."

I smiled. "Nothing to be sorry about, but that was quite an entrance."

The man smiled. "Thanks. I take pride in never arriving unnoticed. Nice store. Yours?"

"Thanks. Yep, it's mine. I'm Harvey." I put out my hand, and he shook it.

"Davis." He moved toward the door. "Sorry again, but maybe I'll come with less fanfare soon and just shop."

"I'd like that. Nice to meet you." I stared as Davis opened the door to the store and turned left toward Chez Cuisine. A small part of me thought about calling Max to let him know a very exuberant man was on his way, but that small part didn't triumph over the larger part who kind of wanted to see Max squirm. Davis had been nice enough, but something about his urgent need to see Max told me this wasn't going to be a gathering of old chums.

Marcus was in one of the front windows straightening our display, so I caught his eye and said, "I'm headed to lunch if you've got it."

"Got it, Boss," he said with a grin. He knew I hated when he called me that.

"Thanks, Assistant Manager Dawson. Be back in an hour." I grabbed my phone and headed out toward Max's restaurant. I didn't want to miss the show.

For the second time in a week, I walked into Chez Cuisine of my own free will. This time, though, I wasn't going to stay long. I had quickly devised the excuse that I needed to talk with Symeon about Mart's birthday in a couple of weeks if anyone asked why I was there.

But when I came in, I was not even noticed. Davis was at the end of the bar, and Max was leaning over having a very quiet, very intense conversation with him. The hostess and the wait staff were clumped in a corner, all eyes on Max and Davis. And the customers were staring intently, too. I suspected Davis had made a repeat performance of his grand arrival, and it was drawing all the focus.

I walked nonchalantly through the dining room and past the bar, giving Max a casual wave as if I strolled into his kitchen all the time. Then, as soon as the swinging door swished behind me, I trotted over to Symeon and said, "What is going on out there?"

Symeon cackled. "I should have known you'd suss out the big story right away, Harvey. I suppose you're talking about the guy who just blew open the door of the restaurant and demanded to see the man who stole away his girl?"

"What?!" I peeked out through the porthole window in the door. "Davis thinks Max stole Lizzie?" I had thousands of questions, but that one slipped out first.

"You know his name?" Symeon asked as he slid slices of mushroom into a skillet full of melted butter. The smell made me glow with pleasure.

"Oh yeah, we're old friends. Go back about five minutes when he blew into my store demanding to see Max." I smiled at Symeon, who was frowning at me.

"Why would he think Max would be there?" Symeon said as he did that things expert cooks can do with flipping and a sauté pan.

I watched with jealousy as I explained about how Davis had seen him the night before and thought maybe he worked at my bookstore, and even as I said it, I realized it was odd.

But Symeon beat my brain to my question. "So he's stalking Max?"

I shrugged. "Sounds kind of like it, huh?" I turned back to the window and looked out just in time to see Max staring at me through the glass. I stepped back, and he slowly opened the door.

"Are you looking for a position here, Harvey?" Max said in a tone that could either be derision or clever snark, but I couldn't tell.

"Um, well, no, you see, I just had to talk with Symeon about Mart's birthday, and you looked busy . . ."

Max rolled his eyes. "Davis told me about coming into your shop. You really are so nosy, aren't you?"

"I prefer the term curious," I said and heard Symeon snicker behind me. "And really, I just wanted to be sure you were okay."

Max grinned devilishly, and I shrank back a little. "So you were concerned about me, were you?" He took a step closer.

"Well, not like that. Just, well, the guy seemed intense." I felt heat rising into my cheeks and wasn't exactly sure what that was about, embarrassment or something else. But I pushed that something else far down into my brain stem and came back to the moment. "So what did he want?" I asked. I figured it was better to just be straightforward rather than pretend I didn't want to know.

Max gestured toward a stool by a tall desk in the corner, and I sat down while he pulled up another stool and sat next to me. We watched Symeon fluff the risotto and then add in the mushrooms before plating the deliciousness and sprinkling it with parsley and truffle oil. He slid that dish up next to a filet of salmon and rang a bell. A moment later, a young woman with purple hair slid into the kitchen, grabbed the plates and stepped back out.

Only then did Max speak. "Apparently, he thought I poached his best bartender."

I scowled at Symeon who smiled mischievously, clearly happy his choice of words had given me the perfectly wrong impression. "Oh," I said, trying to cover up my moment of confusion that Davis didn't think Max had stolen his girlfriend, only his employee. "He owns a restaurant, too?"

"He does," Max said. "A very good one. The Thurber Tavern in Boston. They're famous for their gourmet burgers that are perfectly paired with choice cocktails."

"That sounds amazing," I said before I could stop myself. "Have you been?"

He smiled. "Yep. I go every time I visit the city."

I leaned back on the stool. "You, Max Davies, of the French cuisine, go to a burger joint on the regular." I laughed. "Color me pleasantly surprised."

"I wouldn't exactly call The Thurber Tavern a 'burger joint,'" Symeon chimed in. "Those burgers cost forty dollars a pop."

I nearly fell off my stool. "Forty dollars for ground beef. Really?" Then, I checked my cheap-o mindset and said, "Is it worth it?"

Both Max and Symeon nodded vigorously. "So noted," I said. "I'll plan to check it out next time I'm in Boston." I looked over at Max who was smiling at me with a little gleam in his eye. For some reason, that gleam didn't bother me as much today, and I was bothered that I wasn't bothered.

"Anyway," Max said. "Lizzie, um, Cassandra as he knew her, told him she had gotten a job offer that she couldn't refuse here, and she gave two days' notice and left. Davis came down as soon as the weather cleared to see what had happened. He knew our Lizzie was something special, too."

"But you said he didn't know her as Lizzie?" I asked.

"Nope, he looked up the town, scanned our small offering of restaurants, figured out that mine is the only one with a full bar, and looked me up." Max sighed. "The guy didn't know she had died. Thought he might come and ask my help in convincing her to go back to the Tavern."

"What did he say when you told him?" Symeon asked.

"Oh, I didn't tell him," Max said.

Symeon and I both stared, slack-jawed, at Max. "You didn't tell him? Why not?" I was practically shouting. You didn't have a person come across five states to see someone and then hold back that the someone was dead.

Max looked down at his hands and blushed. "I didn't know how. He seemed so kind, and given how wonderful Lizzie was . . ." He just stopped talking and stared down at the floor.

I put a hand on his shoulder and looked over at Symeon, who was, apparently, as puzzled as I was by Max's newly found conscience. "What did you tell him?"

Max stared even harder at the floor, and I felt a twist in my gut.

"Max, what did you tell him?"

"I told him to go back and see you, and you could help him find Cassandra." He turned his eyes up to me and kept his head down like a sad puppy who wanted my forgiveness.

But I was too busy thinking about how to break the news to this dedicated employer that his favorite staff member had been killed. I didn't have time to forgive Max. Which was good because I wasn't planning to do it soon.

"Jerk," I said as I stood up and walked to the kitchen door. "Just pass the buck, Max. Real classy." I tried to slam the kitchen door, but it just swung and hit me in the back of my legs.

5

I was so mad at Max that I didn't know what to do with myself, but I did know I was in no shape to talk to Davis. So I turned left out of Max's front door and walked toward the art co-op. I needed a place to vent, and I headed toward Cate. She was working on a series of photos about Korean-Americans on the Eastern Shore. It was a passion project for her, something to honor her own heritage and dispel the mistaken belief that the only people in this part of Maryland were black or white. She was hanging the show tonight, so I knew she'd be putting final details on the mattes.

When I walked in, my dear friend smiled, straightened her back, and then rushed toward me as soon as she got a good look at my face. "Harvey, what's going on?"

I felt tears prick my eyes and cursed my tendency to cry no matter what strong emotion cropped up. It was a proclivity that drove my dad crazy because, I think, he hurt when I did and didn't know how to help. But despite my self-awareness and a good bit of conversation with therapists about this physiological response to emotion, it still happened. Now, the anger and sadness and a little bit of fear were spilling over out of my eyes.

Cate guided me to a pair of turquoise, mid-century modern chairs in the front of her studio, and I took the tissue she handed me. "Max is a total jerk." I really wanted to swear, but the door to Cate's office was open so I respected the customers.

"Well, yes, but that doesn't tell me exactly what's going on. What happened?"

I looked at my friend and then explained the entire morning from Davis's visit to my spying on Max to Max's refusal to be a grown-up and tell Davis the truth himself. As I talked, I heard the bitterness and fear in my words, and with each sentence, my language became a little less strident, a little less sure of my righteousness. Finally, when I finished the story and looked at Cate, who had listened quietly and squeezed my hand often, I realized something. "Max is grieving, isn't he?"

Cate let out a long sigh. "I think so. I think he's probably also scared."

"Scared to tell Davis what happened?" I could hear the disbelief in my voice at the same moment I registered that I was, in fact, hiding to avoid having to tell Davis myself.

"Yeah, probably." Cate raised one eyebrow. "So maybe cut the man a little slack. He has trouble connecting with people, and he seemed to really like Lizzie. Then, she was dead in his store on her first day. I imagine you can relate a little, right?"

Her voice was soft, but her words went straight to the center of my heart. I could relate. Entirely, given that not just one but two people had died in my own store. I sighed. "Thank you," I said quietly. "I needed to be called out."

Cate hugged me. "I'm not trying to call you out. Max was a jerk to pass this off to you, no doubt. But I expect he did it because he knew you'd know how to handle it."

I gave her a wan smile. "I suppose."

"And for the record, you have every right to be angry with Max." She looked me firmly in the eye. "Every right. But maybe putting that aside for the moment so that you can prepare to tell Davis his friend was killed is the best thing?"

I nodded. She was right. I would address Max's behavior later. Right now, I needed to figure out how to tell a man who had traveled hundreds of miles that the woman he knew had been murdered. The pit in my stomach grew into a softball, and I groaned. "Okay, so how do I tell him?"

"You just tell him, Harvey. Don't overthink it. Just tell him." She pulled me to my feet. "Want me to come with you?"

I looked at the disarray in her studio, all the half-framed images on her table and the photographs leaning against the wall. "No. You finish hanging your show. I've got this." I walked to the door of her studio. "I'll text you to let you know how it goes."

She blew me a kiss, and I walked out the door, far less angry and far more sad than I had been when I came in. But the brisk, cold air outside gave me courage, and I strolled to my shop with determination. By the time I reached the door, I almost hoped Davis would be there, both so I could get it over with and because I felt like I knew what to say.

Seeing Max in the cafe as I headed toward the register drew me up short, though. He was facing the door, and as soon as he saw me, he stood up and made his way to where I was standing. He took my hands in his and said, "I'm sorry."

I stared at him, looked down at our hands, and back up at his crisp, blue eyes. "What?"

"I'm sorry, Harvey. I shouldn't have put you on the spot. I was just—"

I interrupted him. "I know. We'll talk about it later. But I realize you were scared and sad, and I get that."

He let out a long slow breath. "Yeah. Thanks." He let my hands drop and looked over my shoulder. "Looks like I'm going to have to deal with my fear and sadness, though."

I turned around and saw Davis coming into the shop. He

looked around and then saw Max and me and came over. "Hi. Do you have a minute?" he asked me.

Max didn't even give me a chance to answer. "Actually, I need to talk to you, Davis. Can we sit?" He gestured toward a cafe table, and when Davis nodded, he walked over, pulled one chair out of the way, and sat down in the other.

I looked around the store, saw Marcus had things well in hand, and pulled the chair Max had moved up to sit between him and Davis. I wasn't excited about having this conversation, but from the way all the blood had drained from Max's face, it looked like he could use a friend. I guessed I was as close as it got.

Davis looked from Max to me and back to Max. "What is going on? Did something happen to Lizzie?"

For a brief minute, I puzzled over his question and wondered if I would presume something had happened to someone I knew if I was in this situation. I figured I would if there was this much rigamarole about it.

"Yes," Max said and took a deep breath. "Someone killed her on the first night she worked for me."

Davis's eyes flew to me, and I nodded. "It's horrible, but it's true. We're sorry." I don't know why I felt like I could speak for Max, but I felt his foot slide over under the table and rest against mine. For some reason, the small motion was comforting, and I left my foot in place.

Max described how we'd found Lizzie, told Davis what Tuck believed about how she was killed, and said that the sheriff was working day and night to catch her killer.

When Max finished talking, Davis stared at him for a second and then put his head in his hands and cried. It was one of those quiet cries where the only sign that he was sobbing was the shaking of his shoulders. I felt torn between leaving him privacy to weep and wondering if he wanted company in this hard moment. I opted to stay, as did Max.

After a few moments, Davis took a long, shuddering breath and looked up at us. "How can I help?"

I sighed and smiled slightly. "Maybe you could tell us a bit about Lizzie, I mean Cassandra. I never met her."

"And I only knew her a little. We didn't even know her real name," Max added.

Davis looked from me to Max and then seemed to gather himself. A small smile played across his face. "Cassandra – she only wanted to be called Cassandra, never Cassie – was amazing. The most determined person I ever knew. We met at a wheelchair basketball game. She'd come to cheer on a teammate of mine who she'd met in an amputee support group, and she cheered with such wild abandon that I don't think anyone in the gym that day missed her. My friend had hoped to date her, but Lizzie had made it clear she wasn't interested in dating, just in recovering from her surgery and getting back to her first love, bartending."

Davis looked out the window. "After the game, we all went back to my restaurant for dinner and drinks, and my friend mentioned that Lizzie had won some bartending competitions back in the day. It was a Sunday night, and the restaurant was closing up. So I gave Lizzie a little challenge – rearrange my bar to its optimum set-up."

I imagined the scene. A quiet restaurant. A group of friends like mine. A couple of bottles of wine. The glow of the lights. I placed Lizzie at the table and could imagine her grin when Davis challenged her. I'd never seen her smile, but all the things I'd learned about her and the ideas I'd formed because of her clear interest in Lizzie Borden made me picture her as mischievous and never one to turn down a dare.

"She didn't even hesitate. Within seconds, she was behind the bar and moving bottles. Within thirty minutes, she had rearranged all my glassware, reordered the liquor on the shelves, and told me I needed to move the dishwasher closer to the end of the bar to make for easy restocking." Davis looked down at his hands. "I have to admit, I thought she was kind of cocky, but darned if the next night, my bartenders didn't say that her changes made everything run more smoothly. I hired her immediately to be my bar manager. Best business decision I ever made."

Max smiled. "I didn't get to see her work very long, but she was amazing at her job."

"Beyond amazing," Davis added. "I've never seen anyone make better drinks and be a better listener to her customers. The legend of the barkeep as confidant wasn't just a farce to Cassandra. She took that work very seriously. My customers loved her." He looked at Max. "So when she left, I didn't understand what had happened. I thought you'd made some kind of crazy good offer." His eyes passed from Max to me and back again like he was searching for an explanation.

Max blushed. "Actually, I doubt I offered her anything near what you were giving her. We just don't have the kind of business you do, and our bar just basically serves the tables. Her talents were definitely going to be underused here. I actually told her that, but she was adamant. She wanted to be in St. Marin's, and she wanted to bartend. So she took the job."

I looked between the two men sitting with me. Both of them had clearly admired this woman, and that made me even more sad over her death. It also made me so very curious about why someone would have wanted to kill her.

Apparently, Max was thinking along the same lines because he asked, "Any idea why someone would want her dead?"

Davis shook his head slowly. "Not a single one. Everyone seemed to like her. She had regulars at the bar who came in only when she worked just to talk with her. But I never heard anyone say anything bad about her."

I sighed. No leads there. "Are there other friends of hers that we, um, I mean the sheriff could talk to?"

Davis looked at me for a minute and then glanced out the window again. "You know, beside that mutual friend we had that was in the support group with Cassandra, I never heard her talk about her friends or met any of them. She came to work parties and things, but never with a date or even a plus one."

"Family?" Max asked.

Davis looked at him and tilted his head. "No. I never heard her talk about them either." He glanced down and took a deep breath. "That's weird isn't it?"

I had to admit, it was a little weird, but there were other possibilities, too, including the slim chance that all of this was an act on Davis's part. Maybe he didn't want us talking to other people. Maybe he was just here to see what we knew. I didn't get that feeling from him, but he could have been an excellent actor. "Maybe," I said casually. "Or maybe she just didn't talk about her private life at work."

Davis shrugged. "Maybe." He pushed back from the table. "I'm going to be in town another day or so. Could you give the sheriff my number, tell him I'm happy to answer any questions he has?" He slid a business card to Max.

Max put it in his breast pocket. "Sure thing. And maybe you could help me with the funeral?"

I looked at Max. It was a kind gesture, but an odd one given that Lizzie didn't know anyone here. But then, if we didn't know where her family was, and Davis was the only friend we had contact with . . . And of course it would fall to Max to organize it since he knew her best. I flushed that I hadn't even thought of that.

Davis nodded. "Sure. I can't stay past the weekend, but maybe we could arrange it for Thursday? Or is that too soon?"

Max stood, and the two men moved to the door making plans for a service on Thursday.

Just as he passed through the front door, Max turned back

to look at me. "Thank you," he said. "Talk to you later?" His voice was timid but hopeful.

I nodded and felt a wave of discomfort pass over me, but this time, it wasn't at the thought of talking to Max. Just the opposite, and I didn't know what to make of that.

SOON AFTER MAX and Davis left, we got a flurry of customers, and Marcus and I spent the next two hours recommending books – including suggesting a series of mandala coloring books from Dover to an IT support agent who needed something to do while on the phone with customers. When we hit another lull, I stepped into the back and gave Tuck a quick call to share what Davis had told us.

"Oh yeah, Max already came in. Caught us up. But thanks," the sheriff said. "How's that 'I don't want to talk to Max' thing working out?"

I flushed. "Well, it has turned out to just be easier to talk to him." I felt the deception in my words, but it wasn't a complete lie . . . and right now, I couldn't deal with the complete truth either.

"Uh-huh," Tuck said quietly. "You do what you need to do, Harvey. Be kind about it. But do what you need to do."

Suddenly, I realized, we weren't talking about Lizzie's murder anymore. I could barely swallow.

I HEADED out about four as per usual on the days when I opened the store. I thought about swinging by Daniel's garage and seeing how his day had been, but I wasn't excited about talking with him yet. I wasn't sure why, and I figured that until I did know I needed to stick with our arranged meet-ups. I didn't want to say anything I'd regret.

I decided to take a walk instead and was glad I had brought

Mayhem's sweater along. For Christmas, Henri had knitted my hound girl an orange sweater from alpaca yarn. She said it was left over from a project, but I was pretty sure that this gift was a way of Henri having a dog without having dog fur that might stir up Bear's asthma. The sweater slid snugly over Mayhem's torso and then buttoned at her throat, and the dog loved it. When she saw me take it out, her entire body wiggled so much it was hard to get the sweater on.

But once she and I were bundled up, we headed out, ducking through the parking lot between my shop and the garden center and heading out onto the residential streets that bordered Main Street. At this time of day, children were spilling out of school buses, and I could see golden light coming through the front windows of the old Victorians and quaint cottages along the road. We passed a few other folks and their dogs walking, and Mayhem sniffed with delight when we met a young girl walking her very rotund Russian Blue Cat, who she proudly told me was named Alexander after the tsar. I made a note to check with her mom, who was a frequent customer, to see if she knew Rita Mae Brown's Mrs. Murphy mysteries and the Russian Blue co-star named Pewter.

As I walked, I fought to keep my mind off Daniel – and off Max – and on Lizzie's murder. Clearly, someone had followed her here to kill her. Tuck had said her lease only began last week, and given that none of us had seen her around town, it was clear she hadn't been in St. Marin's long enough to make that kind of enemy of a person from here.

What I couldn't figure out was why someone would want to kill a woman who seemed so good and so, well, quiet. None of my internet searches had turned up anything beyond the bartending competitions she'd won, and Tuck said she had no criminal record. Her social media pages showed a few political posts, although nothing extreme by any definition, and a few photos of nature or new cocktails she was trying out. But no photos with friends or family, which seemed to support Davis's words about her. All in all, what we knew of her gave me very little to consider when it came to the motive for killing her.

Which meant I had no further trails for my mind to go down, and so I spent the rest of the walk wondering exactly why, when Max's foot had shifted against mine in the cafe, I hadn't moved my leg away.

6

B y the time I got home, I had worked my mind around to absolutely no clarity about the men in my life, even that phrase caused me angst, so as I took off Mayhem's sweater and hung up my peacoat and Mart's latest scarf for my ever-growing "Mart-made collection" I decided that clearly my problem was hunger.

I set out the ingredients for a good old chicken and rice casserole and was grateful Mart had caved on her "no processed foods" rule to let me keep one can of cream of mushroom in the pantry. I prepped the parts of the casserole, filled the 9 x 14 pan, and popped it in the oven. I already felt better. I started to pour myself a glass of wine but opted for vanilla chamomile tea instead and had just sat down in my reading chair when my phone rang. Daniel.

My stomach plummeted, and I regretted that I had skipped the wine. But then I realized I liked Daniel. Loved him even. So why not talk to him? I almost had myself convinced when I finally answered. "Hey Stranger," I said.

"Hi," he answered warmly but without any vim. "Just wanted to check in since I didn't see you the past couple of days."

I thought back and realized he was right. It had been a couple of days since we'd talked, probably the longest we'd gone without talking since we met. I felt kind of bad about that but not sad. Guilty maybe.

"Wow, yeah, you're right. Sorry about that. I've just been caught up in everything I guess." I sounded lame even to myself, but Daniel didn't seem to notice.

"Yeah, me, too." There was an edge to his voice, something not quite there about it. "Listen, I want to talk about something with you. Dinner Friday?"

"Sure," I said as my heartbeat quickened. He didn't sound angry or upset. Just distant, and I wasn't sure what to make of that. "Pick me up?"

"Um, well, can you meet me in Easton? That Italian place you like?"

Daniel and I had never met up at a restaurant before. Not once, so I knew something was up. I hated when things were unsaid, and part of me wanted to press him to tell me what was going on. But since I didn't know what was going on with me anyway, I figured another couple of days to sort things might be good. "Okay. Six?"

"Great. Give Mayhem some ear scratches for me."

I ended the call and sunk back into my chair. I thought maybe I should be upset, but mostly, I was just puzzled . . . about a lot of things. I made another concerted effort to put the whole situation out of my mind and let myself escape into my newest read, *A Pedigree to Die For*, a cozy mystery recommendation from Galen that starred Standard Poodles. I felt myself missing Taco as I read and wondered, for a brief second, what it meant that I missed the dog and hardly thought about the man. Then, I disappeared into the world of dog shows and forced myself to forget.

When the timer on the oven went off, Mart walked in the door, as if the bell was ringing her home, and I was so glad to see her. I needed a friend tonight, one who got me, and who would always have my back, no matter what hair-brained thing I did. She slung her bag onto the counter and said, "That smells amazing. What is it?"

"Chicken and rice casserole. I'm just putting the peas on now." I took the bag from the freezer and dumped the veggies into the boiling water. "Tea or wine?" I asked as I turned back to my best friend.

"You're having tea, so I'll join you." She hung up her coat and threw her handmade hat into the top of the hall closet. Then she plopped onto a barstool, picked up the steaming mug I handed her, and said, "Comfort food and cozy tea. What's up?"

I sighed. "Can I tell you the real answer to that question after we talk about Lizzie?"

Mart shrugged. "Sure. So what's up with Lizzie?"

I told her about Davis and about what I'd seen – or not seen – in Lizzie's social media presence. "It just feels weird, you know? Like there's just something really big we need to understand for everything to make sense."

"Yeah, like why does a successful woman who works for a really amazing restaurant in Boston move to our town and assume a name?" Mart asked with a raised eyebrow.

"Precisely." I put down my fork on my clean plate and said, "I know I'm only supposed to be investigating the Lizzie Borden part of this, but—"

Mart interrupted me, "But you can't help it. You want to know more." She smiled. "You love people, Harvey, and you love a good story. Lizzie seems like she was a good person with a great story. I can see why you're getting drawn in . . . but." She looked at me.

I sighed. I knew there was going to be a but. "But this is a murder investigation, and I need to let the police do their job.

Mart nodded. "Ding. Ding. Ding. Of course, I know you

won't do that, but what kind of friend would I be if I didn't at least try to dissuade you from this path?"

"Not a friend at all," I said as I cleared our plates. "I hear you, though, and I'm not asking questions, at least not beyond you and Max."

Mart lifted her eyebrow again at the mention of his name but said nothing.

"But I keep wondering what would make me run and hide. I mean I know about leaving some place and starting over, sure, but to leave and totally disappear?" I put the dishes in the dishwasher and then stood up and stretched my hands over my head. "Seems like the only thing that would make me do that was fear."

"Agreed." Mart got two wine glasses down. "People don't just give up everything from their own lives unless they have to. Do you think she was in WITSEC?"

"WITSEC? Who do you think you are Maggie from *FBI?*" I laughed. "And does that make me Omar because I'm okay with that?"

"If you are him, you don't get to date him, Harvey."

Mart was laughing, but I also saw a glint of something in her eye. And I wasn't ready to talk about that yet. "Good point. Although I do enjoy my own company. But no, I don't think she's in witness protection. I'm sure Tuck has already thought of that."

"So then let's imagine why we might leave. Scary ex? Crime? Blackmail?"

I took the glass of Chardonnay Mart had just poured me and went back to my reading chair. "All of those are possibilities, I guess. And maybe she had to come to a small town. I mean I hate to say it, but news of a really good, one-armed bartender would travel fast in a city. In a town with only one bar, though . . ."

Mart sipped her wine. "Plus, Lizzie probably couldn't know

this, but St. Mariner's gossip but only amongst ourselves. We're fiercely protective. If she'd only been here a little longer, we might have been able to keep her safe."

I felt my sadness over this young woman's death sink deeper into my chest. Mart was right. If she'd made it a few weeks, she would have already had friends, or at least allies, here, and we would have had her back. "But she didn't make it that long," I said, and something lit up in my brain. "But that's it, isn't it? She had only just arrived, and still, someone found her and killed her before we could get to know her."

"Like they were afraid of what she might say." Mart bent before the fireplace and laid newspapers, kindling, and logs out. "She never stood a chance."

My phone rang on the coffee table, and I let out a little yip of frightened surprise. Guess I was edgier than I thought. I picked up the phone. "Tuck," I said to Mart and swiped to answer.

"Harvey, I wanted to give you a heads up. Lizzie's, I mean Cassandra's, mom is in town, and she's asking a lot of questions, not too kindly I might add. I think you can expect her at the shop tomorrow since I gave Marcus a heads up and told him to close a few minutes early tonight."

I glanced down at my watch. Six forty-five. "Thanks, Tuck. Rocky is there with Marcus, right? I don't want either of them getting ambushed alone."

"I'm here, too," he said, and I heard the slurp of a hot drink through the line. "I'm staying until they close up."

He must really be worried then. "Okay. Come by in the morning and prep me?"

"Sure thing. I'll be here at nine thirty. But don't turn the lights on until I arrive. No need to give her a head start."

"Aye, Aye, Captain," I said and hung up.

"What was that all about?" Mart asked.

"Apparently, Lizzie's mom is here, and she's scaring Tuck. "

"Must be pretty terrifying then. I don't think I've ever seen him scared," Mart said as she fed a bit more kindling into her now crackling fire.

I sighed. "Yeah, and apparently, she's coming to see me. As if I didn't already have enough on my mind . . ." I let my voice trail off, unsure about whether I really wanted to have this conversation or not.

Mart had no such hesitations though and launched in. "Okay, so Daniel . . ."

I sighed, and then I spilled. We talked late into the night, and when we were done, I wasn't sure what to do in three days, but I knew what I had to do in two. The thought of it made my chest hurt.

THE NEXT MORNING, Mayhem and I went into the store through the back door just in case Lizzie's mom was out front. I'd only gotten a few hours' sleep, and I really didn't need a confrontation before I'd even had caffeine. On my way in, I'd texted Rocky to suggest she do the same, and she came in right behind me.

"I guess this woman's a force," she said.

I shrugged. "Tuck say anything else last night?"

"Nope, just that she was a short, white woman with purple tips in her hair and that she wasn't interested in hearing anything but what she wanted to hear." Rocky shook her head. "It's going to be a fun Thursday."

I sighed. "Indeed. I just loving being asked questions that someone thinks they already have the answers to. It's my favorite." I pulled a headband into my unruly curls and started up the register in the semi-dark of the winter day. I wasn't about to bring on this woman's interrogation by turning on the lights, so I scuttled around in the shadows tidying up the shelves and waiting for Tuck.

He arrived a few minutes later, via the back door as well, and we settled into the dark corner of the store near the history books and away from the front windows. "The longer this skulking continues, the more I'm going to think this woman is an assassin," I said as Tuck and I held our warm lattes in our hands. "All this cloak and dagger."

"Kind of ridiculous, isn't it? But really, she's relentless. She had me trapped in my office for over two hours while she blasted me with a barrage of questions about the investigation, about why her daughter was in this, and I quote, 'God-forsaken, BFE of a place,' and what I would do when she ruined my reputation as a police officer."

"Good gracious. Who is this woman? And can she do that? I mean is she someone that people listen to, like Batman or something?"

Tuck laughed. "She drove away in a Toyota Corolla, and she has nothing on Christian Bale for deep voices, but she does seem to think she has some power and influence. My research on her, though, is that she's simply a normal person, works as an office manager in one of Boston's biggest accounting firms, and has two children, Cassandra and her brother Claudius."

"And is clearly a fan of the classical world." I said. "A prophetess and an emperor. Talk about naming with ambition."

"I thought the same thing," Tuck took a long pull from his mug. "Part of me wants to believe this is just a grieving mother who is channeling her pain into bullying, but I'm puzzled by something."

I sipped my mug and looked over the rim at him.

"How did she know Lizzie was murdered?" Tuck's shoulders dropped.

"You hadn't notified next of kin yet?" I asked without reproach.

"The Boston PD was supposed to do it today as a favor and courtesy. It's sort of a standard thing to try to notify people about a death in person if we can. I've done it for other police forces when people have died here." Tuck sat forward and put his hands on his knees. "But yeah, they were going this morning."

"So someone told Mrs., um?"

"Mrs. Leicht."

"Someone told Mrs. Leicht." I sat back and let my mind bounce from idea to idea. "Could it have been Davis?" That seemed most likely since he might have at least known Lizzie's parents' names.

"Nope, Mrs. Leicht was on a flight down here yesterday morning."

I pushed my head back into the seat. "So before Davis even knew that Lizzie, er, Cassandra, was dead?" I didn't think I could ever really think of her as Cassandra and wasn't sure I should even try. She had changed her own name after all.

Tuck nodded and sipped his drink. "Something is going on here, and we just aren't seeing it yet. But we will."

I looked at him playfully out of the corner of my eye. "We?" I waggled my eyebrows to press my point home.

"Well," the sheriff sighed. "Yes, we." He looked almost forlorn as he said it, but my heart ticked up a notch.

"You need me to ask Lizzie's mom some questions you can't ask." All morning I'd been pondering what I was going to say to this woman, and somewhere along the way, it had occurred to me that I had an opportunity that the sheriff just didn't – I could be anonymous, at least relatively. No one suspected a bookstore owner to be investigating per se.

"Exactly," Tuck said with yet another sigh. "I need you to find out how she ended up here and why she thinks Cassandra came to town."

"Maybe I can look into the Lizzie Borden angle a little, too, explore that with her mom." My mom would know if I had an obsession with an alleged murderer, and I was betting Lizzie's mom did, too. If she didn't, that might be worth knowing, too.

Tuck stood up but was careful to stay out of the glow cast from the security lights. "Just be cautious, Harvey. We don't want to tip her off that you're working with me."

"Right, that would ruin the point," I said seriously.

"Well, yes, but more importantly, it might put you in danger." He gave me a long stare before he made his way along the shadowed bookshelves and to the back door again.

Now, my heart was really all a-patter, but a quick look at the clock on the wall said it was time to open. Most people in St. Marin's wouldn't notice or care if my store opened a few minutes late, but I was betting a big city woman who was seeking information would definitely notice.

As I walked to the front of the store, I tried to look as casual as possible while also texting Rocky to let her know what was up and to be on standby if I gave the signal, which I had decided needed to be appropriate in context but not too subtle. "If I say, man, 'I miss those peppermint lattes from the holidays,' text Tuck."

"Got it," Rocky wrote back, and when I looked over, she gave me one solid nod. My backup was ready.

And sure enough, as soon as I opened the door, a short, stocky woman with short silver hair tipped in purple bustled in, barely giving me time to open the door. She headed straight for the counter and then corkscrewed her head violently as she looked for someone to help her. Oddly enough, her gaze never landed on me at all, so when I approached and asked how I could help, she frowned deeply.

"I'm looking for some man named Harvey. Owner of this store." Her voice was thick with old-school Boston, or at least I thought it was old-school Boston because that's how Ben Affleck and Matt Damon had talked in *Good Will Hunting*.

"Well, I'm not a man, but I am Harvey, the owner. How can I help?" I tried to sound cordial, easy-going.

She looked at me in the face and said, "Hmph. Well, whatever. I have some questions for you."

Mrs. Leicht was not the first person to dismiss my gender as incidental, but it still stung every time. I could have any name I chose, and I was the gender I was . . . and yet people's expectations about what my name defined about me, well, they were annoying far too often.

"Well, hit me. I love recommending books." I knew I was laying it on a little thick with the unaware bookseller routine, but I didn't want her knowing in the least that I was expecting her.

She glanced around quickly as if noticing for the first time that she was, in fact, surrounding by books and then made a sound like she was going to hock up a loogie before saying, "I don't read." with a smugness that would have been more appropriate for the sentence, "I just won the Pulitzer," or "I just ate the forty-ounce steak at that waterfront place."

"Oh, I see." I let a little disdain slip into my tone because, well, I felt it. It was okay if people didn't read, but being arrogant about it just struck me as ugly.

She either couldn't tell I was annoyed or didn't care because she didn't even look at me as she said, "So you're the one who founds Cassandra's body?"

Now I understood why she wanted to talk to me. If someone I loved was murdered, I'd probably want to meet the person who found them that way, too. But Mrs. Leicht didn't sound like she was here on a mission of grief. Revenge? Maybe? Rage? Definitely.

"I am," I said quietly. "I'm so sorry for your loss. Would you like to go somewhere—"

She cut me off. "So did you kill her?"

I paused, took a deep breath, and then said, "No. I didn't kill your daughter. I didn't even know her."

"Well, that's what you say, but maybe you and she were having an affair, and she realized she could do better." Her tone was acid, and I didn't let anyone talk to me that way.

"Mrs. Leicht, you have just called me both a liar and insulted my value as a romantic partner. Do not speak to me that way." I took another deep, slow breath as she glared at me. "I'd like to help you, but that expression about honey instead of lemons does apply here." I moved out from behind the counter and pointed toward the cafe. "Please, let's sit." No one else was in the store yet, and I knew Rocky would manage the register if need be. For my sake – and for Mrs. Leicht's if she didn't pull it back a bit – I needed to deescalate this situation.

Lizzie's mom glared at me a moment but then followed me to the cafe, where I deliberately chose a seat by the window just so that there would be witnesses. Then, I caught Rocky's eye and asked politely, modeling the tone I appreciated in all my conversations, especially with strangers, "Could we have two decaf lattes, please?"

Rocky smiled and began prepping the espresso. I saw her face sour, though, when Mrs. Leicht said, "What's the point of decaf?"

"With my complements," I said as I glared at my companion. This woman did not need any stimulants. "Now, please tell me what you are trying to find out. As I said, I'd like to help, Mrs. Leicht."

Mrs. Leicht looked at me, seemed to decide something, and said, "I'd like to know what she looked like when you found her."

I was caught up short by the question. I remembered, of course, every detail from Lizzie's body in that moment, but somehow, I hadn't anticipated that her mother would want to hear about that. "Honestly, she looked peaceful."

"That's not what I mean," I could still hear the edge in her voice, but there was also weariness now, too. "Please, just describe her to me."

I looked at the woman a moment longer, tried to think quickly about whether I might be compromising Tuck's investigation, and decided that maybe this hard thing could actually be a kindness. So I described her – the way her body was positioned, how her hair was styled, what she was wearing, even the hot pink lipstick she had chosen for her first shift.

When I finished, Mrs. Leicht seemed puzzled, but it took her a minute to say anything. "But her arm, well, her lack of arm. You didn't mention that."

I studied Mrs. Leicht's face and said, "I didn't. I couldn't see she was missing an arm because of the position she as in. I only learned she was an amputee the next day."

Rocky brought over our lattes, and Mrs. Leicht downed the steaming hot beverage in a single swallow. I wasn't sure how she'd done it, but it was impressive in a fire-eater at the circus kind of way. "Is that important?" I asked after I took my own small sip and discovered it was laced with a delightful hint of cinnamon.

The look she gave me this time wasn't so angry, more inquisitive. "It might be. But not because she was an amputee." I definitely heard a little defensiveness in that last sentence.

I nodded. "I wouldn't think so." I thought back on the disability rights reading I'd been doing and remembered all the times people had said that all abled people saw in them was their disability.

Mrs. Leicht gave me an appraising glance and then sat back in her chair, as if conceding that she didn't need this to be a fight. "Right. Okay, then, well, mostly, I was wondering if you'd tell me you saw a prosthetic arm near her body."

The surprise must have shown on my face because Mrs. Leicht said, "She'd been fitted for a very state-of-the-art one recently, and it's missing."

I tried to stop my brain from leaping to the "so that's why you're here" assumption but wasn't quite successful. "I see," I said to buy myself some time while I thought. I knew next to nothing about prosthetic devices, but I thought they were one-of-a-kind and, thus, not really something worth stealing. But maybe I was wrong. "Are you thinking someone stole it?"

Mrs. Leicht shook her head and the purple tips of her hair swayed just slightly. "Not likely. It was custom made for Cassandra." She paused and then studied my face for a moment as if making a decision. "No, I was wondering if she'd brought it with her. She hadn't really wanted to get it but found she had trouble getting work without it. So she had relented." She looked out the store window at the foot traffic on the street. "When I went to look for her this weekend, it wasn't in her apartment."

Now, it was my turn to interrupt. "You said you went looking for her. Was she missing?"

She nodded. "I hadn't heard from her in over a week. That was unusual. We talked most every day, but recently, her calls had been more infrequent, and she hadn't been picking up when I called. This past week, though, I didn't hear from her at all, and I got worried."

I thought about my mom, about how quickly she'd panic. I'd say twelve hours without hearing from me would probably have her launching a national search. "And when you got to her apartment?" We were making progress here, so I tried to tread lightly. The woman was warming to me, but I sensed I could scare her off if I pressed too hard.

"The arm wasn't there, but neither was she. No sign of her . . . the funny thing was," she studied my face again before continuing, "it didn't really look like she was gone either."

"You mean nothing was really missing? Not like she'd packed to move or something?"

"Exactly. It looked like she'd gone to the store and would be back soon." The anger from before was now morphing into something more tender, more achy. "I'm the co-signer on her lease, so the landlord told me she was paying her rent and had paid ahead by three months. But he hadn't seen her for a week either."

"So then you went looking?" I had to rein myself in, keep from charging ahead with my questions.

"Yes, I had no idea where to look, so I checked everything online. I went through every like, every posting, and finally I came across a mention of this town on a page she'd liked. It was the only lead that seemed out of place. So I followed it, and here I am." She looked at me for the first time like a woman who needed something, like a grieving mother.

I reached across the table and put my hand over hers. "That must have taken hours. I looked at her pages, too, but I never did figure out how she found us here." I felt that tug about the back of my brain, that nudge to pay attention because something needed attending, but I didn't have the space in this moment to think about anything else. I just had to hope some of my brain would keep working while I followed this conversation carefully.

Mrs. Leicht's fingers squeezed around mine. "So you have been looking?" The plea in her eyes was intense.

"Oh yes, everyone here has. We didn't know your daughter, but she was a St. Mariner, and that counts for something here." I felt the emotion snag in my throat.

She let out a shuddering gasp and then said, "Why?"

I put my other hand over hers. "We don't know. But the sheriff, Tuck, he's the best. Really. He has barely slept since we found Lizzie's body."

"Is that the name she was using? Lizzie?" A light came into her eyes.

"Oh yes, I'm sorry. It's the only name we had until yesterday, and so I'm afraid I think of her as Lizzie. But for Cassandra,

Tuck has been chasing every angle. Even has Max and I helping out." I felt like I was probably treading a fine line here by revealing that Max and I were doing research. I was taking more of a risk in exposing Max and me than was maybe necessary, but I tried to do what I would want people to do for me in the same situation. If someone I knew had been murdered in a town where she knew no one, I would want to hear everything.

"Max, that rude man from the restaurant is helping?" She looked skeptical, and I couldn't blame her. Max, on the surface at least, didn't inspire a great deal of warmth or confidence.

"Yes, he is helping. He really liked your daughter. Thought she was the best bartender he'd ever seen, and not just because she could pour a great drink. He said she really listened." I thought back to the way Max had looked when he'd told the story of the patron who never talked or ordered food. He had been wistful, and I wonder if he related to that man, if he wished he had someone like Lizzie to talk to.

Mrs. Leicht asked, "How are you two helping? Are your private investigators or something?" Her tone was a little skeptical, which felt wise.

I laughed. "No, not at all actually. Just nosy neighbors with a penchant for research and information. We were looking into the name that *Cassandra*," I slowed down to make my brain associate that name with the young woman whose story I was desperate to understand, "chose to use here. Maybe you can guide us a little. She went by the name Lizzie Bordo."

A small smile spread across Mrs. Leicht's face, and I took a deep breath. "That's the name she chose, huh? Figures." She sat back and dropped her hands into her lap as she gazed out the window for a few minutes before she spoke with the wistfulness of memory. "When Cassandra was fourteen, our neighborhood association decided to enact a policy that teenagers couldn't trick or treat. 'Too raucous and inappropriate' the announcement said."

Mrs. Leicht's face was practically glowing with tender emotion. "Well, Cassandra was never one to be told what to do – she gets that from me," she said as she met my gaze, "so she decided she was going to trick or treat, and her costume was going to be outright raucous and inappropriate. She fashioned a Victorian dress out of a turtleneck, a doily and an old prom dress she got at a thrift store. Then, she stuffed some of her brother's clothes and crafted a head and arms out of my old pantyhose. But the piece de resistance was the papier-mâché axe she embedded in the doll's chest. It looked very real, and when covered in theatrical blood that she got from a make-up artist I knew, it was gruesome."

I could picture a young Cassandra, all petulant with her dark, sleek hair and fair skin in that high collar as she strolled around the neighborhood. I liked this woman more and more. "I take it the neighborhood association didn't appreciate her act of rebellion?"

"No, they didn't. Even tried to fine her. But Cassandra insisted it wasn't a costume, just self-expression. The next year, every teenager was on the streets with little signs on their backs saying, 'This is my act of self-expression.'" Mrs. Leicht looked at me again. "I couldn't have been prouder."

"Your daughter sounds like an amazing person." Again, I found myself wishing I'd known her.

"She was, she really was. I don't know a person who would want to hurt her. That's what's so puzzling about this." Now, all that rage that was bouncing against me before was washing through the air as sorrow. "Do you have any leads?"

I so wanted to tell her about Davis, about Galen's friend Effie who had come to town from Boston, but I knew that would be crossing a line. So instead I said, "Nothing firm, but the more we know, the more we can find who did this. Can I ask you one more question?"

Mrs. Leicht nodded.

"Bordo? I mean it's close to Borden, and Borden would have been too obvious, but for a bartender to choose a variant of the spelling of a wine?"

"Oh, that's easy. Cassandra hated wine, so I expect that was tongue-in-cheek." She smiled again.

I laughed. "Okay, don't tell Max though. He has some vision of her being a Francophile who appreciates fine vintages."

Mrs. Leicht said, "Deal. But maybe steer him away from that idea so he uses his research time on more productive angles." She stood, and I rose with her.

"Consider it done." We walked back into the bookstore, and I saw that Marcus had come in and was talking to a young father and his toddler son about the Carl board books. "I'm always here, Mrs. Leicht. If you need anything or just want to talk, please don't hesitate. And if you think of anything the sheriff might need to know for his investigation?"

"I'll definitely let him know." She turned to go but then looked back. "Actually, could you tell him about the prosthetic arm? That might be important, but I'm too tired just now. I just want to go and lay down."

"Absolutely." I walked with her to the door and took her hand in both of mine for a minute. "I'm sorry I have to ask this, but it's important. How did you know your daughter was murdered?"

Mrs. Leicht looked at me with confusion. "I didn't. Not when I got here, but when I checked into the hotel, the clerks at the front desk were talking about how a woman with one arm was killed in town." Tears welled in her eyes. "Hell of a way to find out." She let out a shuddering breath and went through the door.

I watched her walk toward a rental car parked on the street and then picked up my phone and called Tuck.

7

I had no idea what to make of what Mrs. Leicht had told me except that it was clear that Lizzie had disappeared from Boston on purpose and quickly. She clearly didn't want anyone to follow her, and only someone as diligent as a mother – or a would-be murderer – could have figured out where she was. Something about that fact was bugging me, but every time I tried to chase down the thought, it ducked behind another one and hid.

So I left it up to the professionals. It took Tuck's two deputies three hours each before they finally found the Facebook page with mentions of quaint towns on the East Coast to see Lizzie's response to someone's post about St. Marin's. "Is it quiet and secluded?" was her question, and the man who had posted originally said it was.

She had asked her question months ago and only acted on it now. But clearly, something had been brewing in this young woman's head for a long time. Now, to figure out what.

I would have spent the whole afternoon spinning about that question if Mom hadn't come in to take me to lunch so we could talk about our fundraising event for NDRN. We weren't publicly announcing that the event was spurred by her murder, but everyone involved knew the impetus.

Mom had decided on a casual evening at the local roller skating rink because it was the largest space available on short notice and because it was the one spot in the area that had made every effort to be accessible to as many people as possible. The rink was wheelchair accessible and allowed chairs on the rink floor, and Mom was excited to tell me about how the rink owners hired guides for blind people so that they could skate freely without fear of running into anyone. They also provided rhythmic lights for the deaf but avoided strobe lights in case someone had a seizure disorder. The place sounded amazing in every way, but I was surprised that Mom was going for something so laid-back. She was usually more of a cocktail dress and tux kind of woman.

"Well, our speaker for the evening pointed out to me that often the most everyday things are often inaccessible to people with disabilities, and so I went on a hunt to find something fun and simple that we could ensure was available to everyone. Roller skating sounded like it." Mom looked pleased as punch, and I was glad. She really was in her element with this event-planning stuff.

"Well, I guess I'll do my usual from my teenage years and hug the wall for the first two hours and then, about the time I get the hang of skates and push off, the event will be over." I grinned at Mom.

"Harvey, you have many gifts. Coordination is not really one of them, but I've always admired your willingness to try anything, especially if it's to help someone else." Mom leaned over and kissed my cheek. "Now, let's talk money."

Mom's fundraising ideas, beyond tickets, included food – Lu, Lucas, and Rocky's mom, Phoebe, were on tap for that – a cash bar that Stephen and Walter would staff, and a silent auction featuring accessible devices, software, and tools as well as the usual books, gift baskets, and stays at people's time-shares. Her hope was to raise five thousand dollars through these things as well as bring in some larger checks through personal calls and letters.

"That all sounds amazing, Mom, but you mentioned a speaker. Who is coming?" I could tell by the way Mom had held back this tidbit for last that she was excited. She was nothing if not a showperson.

She shrugged in an expert performance of modesty and said, "Oh, a friend of a friend had a connection with Annie Segarra, and she said she'd speak."

The name rang a bell, but fortunately, I didn't have to dredge into my memory banks for too long before Mom filled me in. "She's a disability rights activist who is amazing. Funny. Smart. And she advocates for body positivity and LGBTQ+ rights, too. You really need to follow her Insta page."

I laughed. My mother had just said "Insta." "Okay, I will. She sounds amazing. Quite a coup there, Mom." I held up my hand, and my mom didn't hesitate to give me a high-five. Who was this woman?

"She has a really big following, too and said she'd help spread the word. I think we'll sell out." Mom said as she gathered up the baskets from our greasy burgers and fries. Mom knew good food in all its forms, something I was glad I had inherited from her. "Tickets go on sale tomorrow. Can I list your shop as a purchase location? Annie said she'd send a few dozen of her #thefutureisaccessible T-shirts for you to sell.

"Of course. But the event is Wednesday. Is that too short a timeline?" We'd had great events that we pulled together in a matter of days, but this one might be a harder sell given the topic. It seemed to me that the rights of disabled people were still pretty unrecognized at best and labeled as "buck up and make do" at worst. I just wasn't sure we could drum up enough enthusiasm in less than a week.

"We only have three hundred spaces available because of fire code, but I'm launching, with Galen's help of course, a big social media campaign today. So I think we'll have it under control. Just be ready for a big crowd in the morning."

I was still a little nervous, but if Mom was determined, anything could happen. "You got it." I made a mental note to be sure to ask Marcus if he could come in early tomorrow. "Thanks, Mom. This is going to be great."

"Now, let's talk about you." Mom leaned back in her chair and gave me her most motherly look. I felt something give way in my chest, and I started to cry.

"Oh, Harvey, I knew something was wrong. But what is going on?" She had stretched her hands across the table to hold mine.

"I don't really know, Mama. It's just Daniel . . . and Max." My voice broke into shuddering gasps, and I couldn't continue.

Mom stood, picked up my phone, and helped me to my feet. "This sounds like a walk and talk kind of thing."

I gave her a weak smile of gratitude for saving me from further embarrassment in front of our fellow burger lovers and let her lead me to the door. Outside, the brisk air immediately alleviated some of the tension in my chest, and I started to get control of my crying. But it didn't stop, and I didn't need it to. My mom was here, and she was listening.

"So Max has been interested in you for a long time, my daughter, are you starting to be interested in him?" Mom's voice was neutral, but her face was soft and open when I looked at her as we walked along the strip mall sidewalk.

"I don't know. Maybe, but maybe not. I really don't know. But Max is sort of the secondary point, the larger one is Daniel. He's such a good guy, and he's good to me . . ." My voice faded because I didn't know what else to say.

"He is, Harvey. But good to you doesn't mean good for you, and if you're unhappy with him, then it's only fair to tell him."

Mom took my hand under her arm as we continued to walk across the parking lot entrance into a tree-lined park. "Have you talked to him yet?"

I shook my head. "We're having dinner tomorrow." I walked a few steps and then stopped and looked at my mom. "The thing is, Mom, I get the sense that he feels the same way, maybe. He asked for us to talk, I mean, so maybe . . ." I started walking again. "Or maybe that's just wishful thinking."

"Could be either, but you'll know tomorrow." She patted my hand as we watched the birds skitter between the trees. "That feels like forever away, though, huh?"

"Two forevers actually." I was not a patient person. I'd always been one to want to simply make a choice and live with the consequences. Waiting and overthinking made me feel a little unstable. "But at least I have the fundraiser to focus on."

Mom nodded. "Exactly . . . and tonight, you and Mart are coming to dinner with your dad and me. We'll do it up right. Appetizers, drinks, dessert – a long drawn-out meal to help you spend the evening."

I smiled and felt tears start to well in my eyes again. Sometimes kindness was the hardest but most important thing. "Thank you," I whispered.

"Anytime, my dear. Now let's get you back to work." She steered us toward our car and put on soft music while I cried for a few miles.

IN FRONT OF MY STORE, I took a minute in Mom's car to compose myself, let her kiss my cheek, and then steadied myself to go back to work. We had a lot to do to prep for the fundraiser, including updating our selection of books and creating a T-shirt display, and I was so grateful for the distraction.

After I texted Mart to let her know about dinner that night and the reason for it – and read her quick, "Good plan. Pick you up at four?" – I talked with Marcus about how to set up for tomorrow morning. He suggested a table near the door where we could set up with a small cashbox and our mobile credit card reader. That way, people could buy tickets or T-shirts easily, and we could keep the regular register open for book customers, with both spaces able to handle any purchase.

I asked him to get the table and display space for the shirts set up while Mayhem and I made a visit to Elle to borrow a table cloth and ask if she had any flowers we could use to decorate. I knew January was not typically the best season for blooms, but Elle's heated greenhouse let her keep ahead of the competition when it came to winter wedding bouquets. I knew she'd have something amazing.

I wasn't wrong. As soon as I walked into her shop, I smelled sugar and cinnamon and saw the most gorgeous bouquets of silver and white flowers in her cooler. I expected those were for a weekend wedding but hoped she'd have a few stems leftover for our table. "Hey woman," I said, trying to sound more cheerful than I felt. "I'm wondering if you could help me."

Elle was in her backroom, open to the shop floor by a curtained door and a pass-through window, and I could see she was working on what looked like a massive wreath of ice. "I expect so. Give me one sec, Harvey, I just want to get these last few Dusty Miller stems into the wet ring before they start to wilt. Come on back."

I stepped around her counter and sat on a stool by her work table. Elle's fingers moved deftly from stem to wreath and back to the pile of stems. Within a couple of minutes, she had placed the last of her sprigs and held up the wreath for me to evaluate. "What do you think?"

The ornament was gorgeous, all grays and whites like the bouquets, but with tiny, delicate sprigs of glittering silver in between. I wouldn't have been brave enough to use the glitter, but it really set the whole wreath off. "Gorgeous," I said. "A commission?"

"Yep, for your mom, actually." She grinned at me. "She hired me to do the bouquets for her event and asked for something special for the rink's door." She held it up in front of herself and asked, "Big enough?"

I hadn't seen the rink, but the wreath was huge. "I hope so. Otherwise, I'm going to need a permanent assistant for skating. A rink that big might overwhelm my wall-hugging skills."

"Do you think we would put each other in danger if we just tied ourselves together for the night?" She laughed. "At least we'd be able to cushion the other's fall sometimes."

I laughed. "Deal. But I'm also stuffing pillows in my jeans."

Elle laid the wreath down and shook my hand to finalize our arrangement. "What can I do you for?"

"I was actually here to see if I could get some bouquets for our ticket table for the event. Anything you have leftover?" I squinted in an effort to lessen my request at such the last minute.

"Gracious, Harvey. You don't know your mother at all. She already ordered two bouquets and a tablecloth, and she even requested small matching arrangements for the cafe tables. I'll bring them by in the morning if that's okay."

"More than okay," I said with a smile. "Thank you, Elle. Want to join Mart, Mom, Dad, and me for dinner? We're going luxurious, or as luxurious as the Thai place in Salisbury can handle." I knew Mom and Dad wouldn't mind, especially given all the work Elle was doing for her event, and I could use another person to talk with just to keep things light.

"Ooh, that sounds great. I'd love to. What time?" She followed me to the front door.

"Meet at the shop at four?"

"See you then," she said with a wave as I pulled her door shut behind me.

I decided to take my time walking back. Marcus had things well in-hand, and I wanted a minute to ponder both our event next week and Lizzie's murder. I kept thinking about that prosthetic arm. Surely, Lizzie would have brought something so valuable with her. Unless, of course, she didn't want to use it. I didn't know anything about prosthetics, but when I'd had a broken ankle, I sometimes found all the tools – crutches, scooter, a friend's arm – more annoying than just hopping along on my own. Maybe she felt the same way about her arm. After all, from what Max said, she didn't need it to do her job and do it really well.

I had taken the long route along Main Street toward the other end from my store, and it was only when I found myself in front of Daniel's garage that I realized the lights were off. That was strange. He was usually open every weekday and some Saturdays, too. I peered through the high, square windows on the roll-up doors, but there was no sign of life. Taco's bed was even empty. Odd.

I didn't really know what to make of that situation, so I tried to put it out of my mind as I kept on walking. The big question about Lizzie's murder was the motive. So far, nothing anyone had said gave me any clues about why someone would want to kill her. But clearly she had left secretly or else why pay the rent in advance and leave most of her things behind. I'd only do that if I wanted people to think I was coming back soon, that maybe I'd only gone out of town for a couple of days. Lizzie had been running, and she didn't want anyone to know.

My thoughts had kept me distracted and hyper-focused, so I almost jumped out of my skin when Max grabbed my shoulder and said my name, "Harvey. I've been calling you. Are you okay?"

His face was concerned, and I was jarred a second time by his care. "I'm fine. Sorry, I was just thinking about Lizzie."

He nodded. "Me, too. Do you have a minute?" He pointed toward his restaurant door with an urgent wave.

I glanced up the street toward my store and didn't see a throng waiting to burst through the doors. Marcus could handle things a few more minutes, and I really wanted someone to talk with about what I was thinking. "Sure," I said, hoping I wouldn't regret this for any number of reasons.

Max and I walked to the bar, where he poured us each a cup of Earl Grey and slid a cream and sugar set in front of me. I wasn't much of a tea drinker these days, what with the coffee bar in my shop, but I did love a good cup of milky, sweet tea when I was feeling agitated. And I was some kind of agitated these days. "Thanks," I said as I unabashedly put three teaspoons of sugar in my mug. "So what were you thinking?"

"Well, Tuck let me know that the Bordeaux theory wasn't worth pursuing because Lizzie didn't like wine," he rolled his eyes but in a sardonic and playful way that lacked malice, "so I started thinking about the few things she had told me in our interview and brief conversations in the days between when I offered her the job and when she started."

I took a sip of tea and said, "And did anything come to mind?"

"I'm not sure." He stared at the bottles behind the bar before looking at me again. "At the time I didn't make much of it, but now . . ."

"Now, everything seems weighted," I finished. "Hit me. Maybe I can help evaluate whether it's actually weighty or not."

He smiled. "Well, she called one afternoon a couple of days before she was about to start and asked if I would mind keeping her off our Facebook page. She said she wasn't much for having her picture taken and would rather just be anonymous if I was going to make any kind of announcement or anything."

"Do you usually announce your new hires?" I asked. I didn't follow Chez Cuisine's page, didn't spend much time on Facebook at all, so I wasn't familiar with the kinds of things Max posted.

"Not typically, although I did do a big to do for Symeon's arrival because, well, he has a Michelin star." Max blushed, and I wondered if he was embarrassed that he'd flaunted someone else's accomplishment for his own gain or because he had managed to land such a talented chef.

"Ah, so she didn't want you to do the same for her, and she didn't know you weren't intending to?" I could see why this might seem both really crucial and totally unimportant, especially since Max hadn't even thought about sharing news of her arrival. "You probably didn't think much of it at the time because you hadn't been intending to share the news."

"Exactly," he said, and some of the tension slid off his face. "But now, well, doesn't that seem odd? I mean, sure it would help my business if the bar did well, but she'd also benefit if a post like that drew more customers. Better tips and all."

I stared at the bottle of blue liquor whose name always failed me and nodded. "She clearly didn't want her name and face announcing her location. Tuck told you about what Mrs. Leicht said about her apartment."

"He did. Sounds like she left no trace of her leaving much less of where she left for."

I looked over at him out of the corner of my eye. "I think she was running. Far and fast. The question is why."

"And from whom?" Max said solemnly.

We sat in silence for a few moments, and then I said, "Did Tuck tell you about Lizzie's prosthetic arm?"

He spun on his stool and stared at me. "No. She had a prosthetic arm?"

"Apparently, and a really high-quality one, from what her mom said. It wasn't in her room, but I'm presuming you didn't see her wearing it either?"

"No, never. In fact, in the interview she actually asked me

directly if I was okay with her having only one arm." He shrugged. "I told her that as long as she could do the job, I didn't care one way or the other." He looked away from me for a moment. "She seemed pleased with that, I think, like I'd said the right thing."

I could, in my own way, see why that would please her. When business associates found out I was a woman who went by the name Harvey, I was always buoyed when they didn't comment, as if my gender wasn't an issue. It wasn't the same thing as being valued for your skills in a job interview when you had a visible disability, but I felt like maybe it was akin. "So the arm isn't at her apartment, and she wasn't wearing it here. That seems important somehow."

Max nodded thoughtfully. "But how?"

I stood up. "I have no idea, but we don't have to figure that part out. Not our job. I'll let Tuck know." I walked my mug around the bar and washed it quickly in the small bar sink. "Thanks for the tea, Max."

He stared at me and then down at the mug. "You didn't have to do that?"

"I try to clean up my own messes," I said and walked into the cold afternoon feeling a little brighter.

WHEN I REACHED the shop a few minutes later, Mayhem bolted into the warmth and then burrowed into the wool blanket I had added to her favorite bed in the fiction section. She'd been quiet and attentive to all the goings on of the street while I'd been at Elle's and in the restaurant, but clearly, now, she wanted to send a message about how a single sweater was not adequate attire for extended outdoor time. She looked at me with her eyes and nose showing from the blanket she had somehow gotten over herself as if to say, "Take note, woman," and I did.

But I didn't have long to ponder my dog's cold nature

because Effie, Galen's friend, approached me as soon as I got my own scarf and coat off by the register. "I came by to say I read *The Glass Castle* in two days, and it was devastating . . . but in the best way. I had to say thank you."

I smiled and saw the genuine enthusiasm in her face and knew the look: she wanted to talk about the book. *Poor Marcus*, I thought. I left him alone, and now I was going to get caught up in a book conversation. I was going to owe him an afternoon off for sure.

But then he was there beside me with a smile. "Isn't that book amazing? Did you notice how she simply tells the facts of her life and her mother's choices without indicting her mom?"

Effie nodded. "It was incredible. Somehow, even though I realized that a toddler should not be boiling water to cook her own food and that the adults in that house were highly negligent, I was far more fascinated with the child's resilience than with the parents' neglect."

Now, I couldn't help myself. "I wouldn't have been able to be that gracious in her situation, but I think that's what made the book so powerful. It lets the reader come to a place of peace along with Walls while also holding great sympathy, empathy even, for how much the Jeanette in the book must have suffered."

Effie nodded, and I saw a shadow of something pass across her face. Sorrow. Malice. I wasn't sure, but the emotion was dark, very dark, even in the split second it took Effie to slide her readerly face back on. "If I ever write a memoir, I'm going to take her lead. Tell the truth but tell it with an eye toward compassion."

Her dispassionate visage was still there, but I could hear that darkness in her voice still. I glanced at Marcus and saw a furrow of worry in his brow, too. There was something this woman wasn't saying.

"Anyway," Effie said cheerily, "I'm here for more book recommendations."

Marcus leapt into action and only shot me a puzzled shrug after he headed toward the shelves. I tagged along, not because Marcus needed me – he knew more about the books in the store than I did most days – but because I wanted to listen in just in case Effie said anything that shed light on Lizzie's death.

He started off with a couple very popular recommendations, *The Liar's Club* by Mary Karr and *Running with Scissors* by Augusten Burroughs. "If you find the stories of dysfunctional families to be intriguing, these two will definitely fit the bill," he said as Effie took both books from his hands and scanned the covers before tucking both into a stack under her arm.

Then, as if he'd read my mind, he pulled *The Center Cannot Hold* by Elyn R. Saks down and said, "I just finished this one. It's about a woman with schizophrenia and how she came to be a professor and how her illness led her to her work as a psychiatrist. It really made me reconsider my view of people with serious mental illnesses. Until I read this, I hadn't realized how much prejudice I had."

I watched Effie closely as Marcus talked, and while her face mostly read as interested and engaged, each time Marcus mentioned Saks's disability or his own feelings toward it, I saw a little muscle in Effie's jaw twitch. And when he pulled *Laughing at my Nightmare* by Shane Burcaw off the shelf and held it out to Effie, she actually hesitated before picking it up. The cover showed Burcaw in his wheelchair, and it seemed just the image made Effie uncomfortable because she began shifting from foot to foot as Marcus explained how funny the book was but, again, how it changed his views.

"Well, thank you, Marcus," Effie said when he finished his pitch. "These all look great. I'll definitely consider which I'm reading next." She glanced over toward me as I leaned against the next shelf. "I do still have *Calypso* to read, so I might not get all of these."

"Of course, no pressure," Marcus said. "Just let me know if you have any questions." He winked at me as he headed toward a customer in the military history section.

I started to move back toward the register when Effie said, "Have you read this one?" She held Burcaw's book up with the tips of her fingers only, a fact I noticed only because I was a little worried she might drop the book and damage it.

"I haven't, but Marcus has raved about it. Said it was so funny." I sighed. "I wish I could read every book here, though." I gave her my best "What can you do?" look and turned the corner.

A few minutes later, while I was straightening the children's section after what looked like a herd of hippopotami had come through, I noticed Effie at the counter buying two books. After she left, I rushed over. "Nope, didn't buy either of the ones by people with disabilities," Marcus said before I could ask.

"Figures," I said. "Thanks for trying."

He smiled, "Always happy to help, Investigator Harvey." He saluted me and headed toward the cafe for his afternoon latte and catch-up with his girl.

I stared out the window wondering exactly why Effie had such a visceral reaction to conversations about and images of people with disabilities.

8

At four p.m., Mart pulled up to the curb just as Elle arrived at the store, and I waved to Marcus and blew Rocky a kiss. Normally, I felt bad leaving the store at all, but tonight, I knew I needed my people.

I had thought we were going to pick up Mom and Dad at their condo, but when I got into the back seat of Mart's car, Mom was already there. "Oh, Hi," I blurted. "Where's Dad?"

She sighed. "He did his usual and bailed when he heard there were going to be four women. Used some excuse about us having girl time, but really, he just doesn't like to be outnumbered."

"Might be a smart move," I quipped to cover up my hurt. I really needed my dad right now. I needed a man to sit with me and hear me, to take my side. The light buzz of excitement I'd been feeling about the night faded as we pulled out.

Fortunately, a dirty martini and some mozzarella sticks lifted my mood rather quickly, although I still missed Dad, and once we'd caught up on all the news about the fundraiser for DNRN and about how the investigation into Lizzie's murder had gone, the table got quiet. My friends and Mom just sat in the silence for a few minutes before Mart said, "Okay, Harvey, tell us."

I felt tears stinging my eyes, and so I took a huge gulp of my second martini. Then, I said, "I think I need to break it off with Daniel."

I had been expecting gasps or words of shock. But all three of them simply nodded, and Mom said, 'Yeah" in an almost whisper.

"You guys aren't surprised? Why not? I'm kind of surprised." I wasn't sure what to feel – relieved that they weren't surprised or frustrated that they weren't. So I went with neither. "Tell me why this isn't a shock."

Elle went first, which I was grateful for because she was the newest friend in the group and didn't know me that well. Mart and Mom might just tell me what I wanted to hear, but Elle, while kind, didn't know me well enough yet to do that expertly.

"Daniel is a good guy. A great guy. But for someone else. He's reliable. Simple in the best way. But he's also not that curious. He doesn't want to travel, even through pages or music. He's very content to just be who he is where he is." Her voice was clear and solid, and I could hear the truth in it. "You, however, want all kinds of things that stretch you, change you. You are not a woman content to just be. You want to go, not necessarily on planes or ships, but at least in your mind. You need to be free to do that, and I'm not sure you could ever feel free as long as you felt like you were leaving Daniel behind."

Now, I was the one to take a deep, long inhale. Elle was completely right. I hadn't been able to articulate what I was feeling about Daniel – probably because Max was in the mix – but that was it exactly. Daniel was good, but he wasn't curious. I was nothing if not curious. If I separated out my strange draw to Max, I was left with less than great joy about the idea of marrying Daniel, a fact which made me profoundly sad.

"Harvey, do you remember that conversation you and I had

on your birthday just after you and Daniel started dating?" She reached over and took my hand. "We were sitting by the fire in the yard, and you were telling me you liked him but weren't sure."

I sighed. I did remember. "You told me that he was a nice guy, but you had one hesitation: that he and you would run out of things to talk about." I could remember her exact words, had thought about them over the past couple of years, but now, they spoke volumes, volumes I hadn't been able to hear before.

She squeezed my fingers. "I think you've run out of things to talk about."

I swallowed hard.

Mom leaned her stomach against the table's edge and took my face in her hands. "It's okay to just do what you want, Harvey. You don't have to sacrifice your happiness for any reason, not even a promise." She looked down at the ring on my finger. "Daniel will understand, someday maybe, but he will. And darling, if you feel this way, don't you expect he does, too."

I thought about his voice on the phone the night before, the distance in it. Not coldness. Not anger. Not even sadness. Just distance. "Thanks, Mom." I sat back hard against the booth. "I guess I know what I need to do."

Mart took my hand again. "We're here, Harvey."

"Yes, we are," said a voice behind me, and I spun around to see Henri and Cate. "We heard it was going to be a hard night, so we came to live it up with you, help you pass the hours," Henri said.

Cate's voice was kind but exuberant, too, and I felt gratitude swimming out my eyes. "Pull up another table."

"Already in the works," Henri said as Cate helped two waiters drag another table from across the room. The restaurant was getting empty, but the bar would be open for hours yet. I expected our waiter was glad for the padding to his tip.

The women sat down, and Cate leaned her head on my

shoulder. "Do you want to talk more?" She looked up at me, her face open to whatever I needed.

"No," I shook my head and felt my curls bounce around my face. "No, I know what I need to do. I'll fill you all in on how our dinner goes via text tomorrow night." I didn't need to ask how everyone knew. Friends told friends things, even private things, because friends knew that in the hard days, a woman needs all her people. "Mart, though, I'll need some peanut butter popcorn, white wine, and cheese doodles at the ready."

Mart nodded and said, "Already in the pantry."

I laughed, and Henri reached around Cate to hand me another martini. "Drink this and that big glass of water. We want you to have fun tonight but not regret it in the morning."

"Regret what?" a male voice asked, and from around the corner of the bar stepped Stephen and Walter. "Harvey, mind if we join you?"

"Not one bit," I said with a wave of my slightly tipsy hand toward the other side of the new table. "Everyone else will catch you up. I'm eating olives." I slid one of the big juicy ones into my mouth and sat back to see my friends. They had rallied, and while I was desperately sad, they were all here . . . and I remembered that the best moments of life are often perfectly bitter sweet.

We sat around with drinks and a few more orders of mozzarella sticks for a couple of hours. I had one more martini and three more glasses of ice water, and then Mart had to help me to the bathroom before we drove home. It wasn't the best night of my life, but it wasn't the worst either . . . and it could have been that.

THE NEXT MORNING, I definitely felt the effects of the four martinis, but a couple of ibuprofen and a bacon sandwich later, I was feeling pretty good. Well, pretty good except for the knot in my stomach about dinner with Daniel.

I couldn't dwell on that though. I had an event to sell tickets for, and Galen was coming by at nine thirty to interview me on his Instagram stories with the hopes that he'd help bolster the buzz Mom already had going with Segarra. I'd had my doubts, but sure enough, it looked like we'd be in good shape for Wednesday's event as long as it didn't snow again.

When I arrived at the store after a brisk walk to finish clearing my head, the lights were already on, and everyone was already there. And by everyone, I meant "everyone." Stephen and Walter were out front planting fresh winter cabbages that I knew Elle had brought by when she dropped off the bouquets. Normally I hated those plants because people put them in, let them bolt in the warm days, and never tended them. But these were pert balls of purple, and they really did pep up the window boxes Woody had made and that I'd simply been filling with greenery since the holidays.

Woody himself was inside hanging a wood-burned sign above the ticket desk that said, "Tickets Here," and in the cafe, Lucas had set up a table with tiered dishes full of cupcakes. "Another small fundraiser for you, Harvey," he said.

I laughed. "Mom?"

He nodded, and I headed to Rocky's counter for the double espresso latte I had requested via text on my way in. I needed the extra boost. She had it perfectly made in a super-large mug and with a steamed milk "thumbs up" on top. "Thank you," I said and gave her my own thumbs up.

At the register, Marcus was counting cash and sliding change into the cashbox for the ticket table, and from there, I could see that Cate was facing all the shelves so that the spines came just to the edge. Elle was placing small bouquets of flowers on all the side tables near my reading chairs, and Henri was dusting everything in sight. My team was on hand, and I took a deep breath. It was going to be alright. No matter what. It was going to be alright.

A few minutes later, Mom and Dad arrived, and while Mom arranged Serraga's T-shirts and other merch on the display Marcus had created, Dad came right to me. "Honey," he said and put out his arms.

I fell hard against his chest and let him squeeze me tight. "Thanks, Dad. I missed you last night."

Despite being a hard-nosed business man, my dad hated conflict and confrontation – Mom always said he was a quintessential Enneagram 9 – and so he wouldn't meet my eyes. But he did, while staring at Marcus and Mom, say, "Sorry, Harvey. I thought it was just a fun night. If I'd known . . ."

"I know, Dad. Next time, though, maybe come anyway. Women are pretty fun to hang with, and besides, you wouldn't have been the only man. Stephen and Walter were there."

To his credit, Dad looked a little chagrined. "Deal." He hugged me again. "Now, your mother has given me my marching orders – I am to hang balloons outside – unless you need something else in here."

I smiled. "And counteract the balloon operation? No sir." I pointed toward the door. "Anything I need cowers in the face of the helium requirements."

Dad rolled his eyes, and I even winced at my own plodding attempts at humor. Clearly, I needed rest . . . and to have this day over with.

Still, I put on a good face and enjoyed my conversation with Galen and Mom, who I pressured into joining me, and Galen said we had several hundred viewers. He was optimistic it might result in a few sales or at least a few donations to the DNRN. And sure enough, Mom's phone pinged a few moments later to notify her that a sizable donation had been made to her Venmo account in support of the DNRN.

I hadn't even known my mom knew what Venmo was

much less how to use it, but there she was sending emoji gratitude signs back to the donor as she drifted toward the ticket table.

At the kick-offs for the other fundraisers the shop had helped support, Daniel had always been here, and I missed him. But only now did I realize that it was the absence of a friend that I was noting, not the sorrow I might expect if the most important person in my life wasn't part of a big day. It was another hint, another reminder that I was doing the right thing, as hard as it was.

I took a moment and went to sit with Mack and Mayhem, who had taken up prime position in the front window and were already attracting attention. It was 9:50, and a line was forming at the door. Mom had done it again.

In the last ten minutes before opening, I did a quick sweep of the store to make sure everything was shipshape, and I pulled out a couple of boxes of backstock and tucked them under the ticket table so that Marcus and I could refill the window display if needed.

Then, I turned on the neon sign, unlocked the door, and stepped out of the way as the two dozen or so people who were waiting made their way in.

BY NOON, we'd sold two hundred tickets, and by the time we closed up at seven, the event was sold out, thanks in no small part to Segarra's own Instagram story and regular tweets throughout the day. Fortunately, Mom had set up a system to keep the tickets available for people who would be actually attending but that also allowed people to buy "solidarity" tickets to support the cause and to create another means of social media promo for just before the event. She was being cryptic about exactly what she planned to do, but I knew it would be good.

Still, even with the good news about the event, I locked up the shop that night with a heavy heart.

As I walked to my car, which Mart had dropped off for me earlier along with a card to say she loved me and would be at home waiting when I got there, I saw her and Symeon on the sidewalk in front of Max's restaurant. Symeon had his portable pizza oven going, and there was a banner saying, "Support Equality for Disabled People. Buy a Pizza." on the front of their table.

I stopped briefly and said to Symeon, "Mom got to you, too."

Mart came around the table and put her arm around me. "Actually, this was our idea. A way to support you and your good heart." She squeezed me, and I took a deep breath to keep from sobbing.

"Thank you," I said. "You are both amazing." I took another shuddery breath and said, "Text you when I'm on my way back." I handed her Mayhem's leash and turned to go.

"Or I'll come get you if you need me, too." She held up her phone. "I'm all yours tonight."

I waved as I started the car and pulled away from the curb. I would be a total mess – as opposed to the partial mess of the moment – without such amazing friends.

Nothing good was going to come of me stewing over things on the drive, so I turned on the copy of *There There* by Tommy Orange that I'd just borrowed from the library's audiobook app and let myself be distracted by the story of people recovering from generations of trauma and re-discovering their stories. It was a hard book, which meant it was perfect for this night.

I saw Daniel's truck as soon as I reached the restaurant parking lot, and I also saw two long ears hanging and a wet nose against the truck window. I bent over with sorrow. Taco. I was losing Taco, too. All my life, I'd found the love I have for animals to be more pure, more uncomplicated than any I'd had for humans, and so while I couldn't let myself break down for more than a second before dinner, I knew that, later on, it was going to be Taco's face that let me crack open my sadness all the way.

I tapped on the window and let him sniff my fingers through the small open sliver in the window Daniel had left for him. There was a pile of wool blankets on the seat, and I knew Taco – unlike Mayhem – was not hampered by the cold. He'd curl up there and be just fine, especially because I thought our meal was probably going to be pretty short. I knew I couldn't hold what I needed to say long and wasn't even sure I should try to order food.

Daniel had managed to get us a quiet booth in the front corner of the restaurant. It was private, but it also meant I didn't have to snake through a bunch of tables while I tried not to cry. I wondered if this choice had been intentional and once again thought, maybe, he was feeling the same way I was.

He waved casually when he saw me, and I slid into the booth across from him. "Hi," I said, trying to be friendly without appearing overly chipper. I had never understood those scenes in movies where the person at the restaurant makes it all the way through dinner before giving the big speech. That felt so false, so dishonest to me.

"It's good to see you," he said, and I could tell he meant it, even though there was sadness in his voice. "It's been a few days."

"It has," I said. "I noticed your garage has been closed. Are you okay?" The fact that I had to ask that question wasn't lost on me. Even a month ago, I would have known if he wasn't, but clearly, something had shifted.

"I am. I'm good actually. But I'm sad, too." He took a sip of his soda and then moved the bowl of homemade potato chips he'd ordered around on the table. "I'm moving, Harvey."

I blinked a few times while I stared at him. I knew something was up, but I had not expected that, not from Daniel. He loved St. Marin's and had a really good business. I was shocked. "Moving? Where?" I could hear the sharpness in my voice, and I hoped it didn't sound like anger. It wasn't, just surprise.

"Damascus." His voice was quiet.

"Syria?"

"No," he smiled then. "Maryland. Do you remember that show *Junkyard Empire?"*

"Maybe. Remind me which one it was?" Daniel loved every auto reality show, and I enjoyed watching them with him because I learned a lot. But to be honest, I had a hard time keeping them straight.

"It's the one where the father and son own a salvage yard and sell parts but also fix-up cars sometimes." There was a gleam in his eye, and his voice was becoming more animated.

"Oh yeah, where they spend money on making cars far uglier than when they started? I remember." I had found the business of the salvage yard fascinating, but they really did make cars ugly. "What about it?"

"I'm going to work on the show." Daniel stared at me, waiting for a reaction.

It took me a minute to process what he said, but once my synapses fired all the way, I took a deep breath and smiled. "You're going to be a on a car TV show? Congratulations." I hadn't thought that television was Daniel's dream, but getting to work on cars without having to contend with customers every day definitely was.

"Well, I won't actually be on the show. I'll be behind the scenes doing the mechanical work." He dropped his eyes to the table. "I'm sorry I didn't tell you sooner."

I felt the lump in my throat lodge at the back of my mouth. "How long have you known?" I still felt sure about what I needed to do, and I expected this news meant my announcement wouldn't hit Daniel so hard. But still, I didn't want to think he'd been hiding this news from me for months or something.

"Since Tuesday." He wouldn't meet my eyes. "I mean, I heard about the position on Tuesday, but I didn't want to tell you until I was sure. I was up there the rest of the week getting the lay of the land. They offered me the job on Wednesday."

The day he'd called me to set up this dinner. Relief flooded my chest. "Oh, Daniel, I really am happy for you. When do you start?" I knew the answer, I think, but I needed to hear him say it.

"Monday." He looked up at me then, and I could see the plea in his eyes. He needed me to be behind this. No, actually, he needed me to let him go.

"Wow. They must really like you." I kept my voice light, and I felt lighter. Still very sad but also truly happy for him. This was his opportunity of a lifetime, and I was so glad he was taking it. "You're moving this weekend?"

"I am." He took my hand. "Harvey, I'm so sorry."

I took a deep breath. Oh my goodness, he was going to break up with me. We were totally about to break up with each other – for different reasons but still . . . "Daniel, I came here to hear what you had to tell me, of course, but I also had something I needed to say. Maybe I could do that now?"

He squeezed my fingers and nodded.

"I think we need to break off our engagement." The words slipped out far more easily than I had imagined. "We just want different things in life, and while you are an amazing person, I don't think we're 'end game.'" I smiled as I said it, hoping he'd get the reference.

"Did you just use a *Riverdale* reference in your break-up speech?" Daniel said with a smirk. "That is impressive." He put both his hands over mine and grew serious. "But I agree. We are good as friends, but yeah, I sometimes feel like I'm holding you back, like you'd live bigger if I wasn't there. I don't want to hold you back, Harvey."

I swallowed hard and took a sip of the Cheerwine he'd ordered for me.

"But I don't want to feel guilty for wanting a simple life." He sat back and laughed. "A simple life on a TV show. I do realize how that sounds."

I laughed, too. "Yep, you and your Hollywood friends just kicking it by a bonfire. I can see it now."

"Well, not a bonfire, but maybe a barrel fire in the junk-yard." He shoved a chip in his mouth and smiled at me. "So, we're okay?"

I sighed. "We are." I knew what I was going to say was about to sound so lame, but I meant it. "Friends, though, right? I don't want to lose that."

"Absolutely," he said, "and I saw tears in his eyes. Always."

"Oh good," I said with a wiggle, "because I need to see how they film that show. I mean is it scripted totally or some improv? Who writes the storylines, such as they are? Does everyone actually work there?"

"Slow your roll, woman. I'll get you on set soon." He grew quiet, then. "But I do have to ask one more thing of you, if that's okay."

The lump was back, but I nodded.

"I can't take Taco with me. The hours are too long, and they don't allow animals on the set. Would you take him?" I could hear the tightness in his voice as he spoke, and I knew this was so hard for him.

The tears poured down my cheeks as I slowly nodded. "I would be honored. And you'll come visit whenever you want, and when I get to do set visits, I'll sneak him in." I was crying so hard that I had to put my face in my hands.

Daniel reached over and grabbed my forearm in a tight

squeeze. "Thank you, Harvey. He and Mayhem are besties, and I know he'll be happy with you, too."

I wiped the tears from my face with a napkin. "He will have a lot of women to contend with, you know, and Aslan will clearly have an issue with his presence."

"Oh, he's used to her, and I think, secretly, he's a ladies' man at heart. He'll eat up all that loving." Daniel's voice cracked, and I could tell he was trying to hold back tears himself.

I took another sip of my drink and said, "Do you want dinner?"

He shook his head. "Well, not unless you do. I'm happy to order something for you."

"No, thanks. I actually think I'd probably like to go now. You know?"

He stood and helped me into my jacket because he did know. He knew me, knew that the emotions were waiting there and would need more release soon. "Taco will be so glad to ride in the Scooby-Roo again."

"Oh, that reminds me," I said as I saw Daniel drop a twenty on the table, "can you keep the truck? I mean we never had it transferred to my name, and I would really like you to have it. Show those people in Damascus what a classy classic looks like." Daniel had bought me a truck a year or so ago, and while I loved it, I barely drove it because I walked most places in town. Daniel, however, adored that vehicle, and I wanted him to have it.

"Are you sure?" he asked. "I bought it for you."

"I'm sure. Scooby and I are good," I said as I opened the door of my Subaru and cleared the passenger seat for Taco.

"Thank you," he said, "for everything." He hugged me tight and then walked quickly to his truck, where he climbed in and spent a few minutes with Taco while I warmed up the car.

Their goodbyes said, the two boys walked over, and Taco jumped into the passenger seat like he knew his girl Mayhem was waiting, and maybe he did. I never would quite understand what dogs knew, but I knew they understood far more than we often gave them credit for.

"Bye Harvey," Daniel said and kissed my cheek.

"Bye Daniel," I whispered as I handed him the engagement ring and pulled the door shut.

I watched him walk back to the truck and start it up, and I started my car and pulled out so that he'd know I was on my way. But then, once he had headed back toward the mainland, I pulled over in a gas station and let myself cry into Taco's ears for a while before I texted Mart. "Taco and I are on our way. Have the cheese doodles ready."

9

W hen I got home, Mart had started the fire, laid out a smorgasbord of junk food, cued up *Making the Cut*, and somehow procured a second dog bed to put beside Mayhem's near the fireplace. Taco came in, greeted Mayhem and Mart, and then curled up and was asleep on his new bed in less than five minutes.

I had no doubt he'd miss Daniel as the days passed – I would, too – but he'd spent enough nights here to be quite comfortable, obviously.

Mart handed me a glass of white wine and pointed out that she also had hot tea for later and then listened as I recounted my conversation with Daniel. When I was done, she said, "Well, it sounds like it went well. Not easy, but well."

I sighed. "Yeah. We were clearly on the same page, and while I still feel pretty sad, I also feel lighter. And I'm really happy for him." I meant it when I said, it too.

A series of images of Heidi Klum and Tim Gunn was carouseling across the screen, and I gestured toward the TV. "This is a perfect choice." Mart and I had begun watching the fashion show the week before, and we were both loving the clothes – for commentary, not as actual wardrobe – and the designers.

"Good. But first, I need to tell you about something that happened this evening." She sat up and put her wine glass on the coffee table. "That guy Davis came by the pizza table just after you left."

"Oh, did he say anything? I thought he was leaving town yesterday?" That's what he'd told Max and I when they'd begun discussions of the funeral. It turned out that they couldn't get everything arranged in time, so the service was going to be tomorrow. "Did he decide to stay for Lizzie's funeral?"

"Maybe. He didn't really say." Mart paused, like she was thinking about my question, but then went on with her story. "He wanted to know what the funds from our pizza sale were being used for specifically, and so I told him about NDRN. I guess I went on a little long because he basically interrupted me and said, 'So do they help people have money for pros-thetics and stuff?'"

I furrowed my brow. "That's a really specific question, and a weird one if you were talking about the lobbying and legisla-tion stuff."

"Exactly what I thought, too. I was talking about all the ways they try to change laws, and he piped up with that. And when I told him I didn't know but he could look on their website, he said, 'Okay, I'll do that.' And left."

"He didn't even buy any pizza?" From my years in fundrais-ing, I knew that if someone stopped, they were already likely to give, and if they talked to you about the purpose of your fundraising, they were almost certain to give . . . unless of course they were turned off by what you told them about the organization or event for which you were raising money.

"Nope. Didn't even drop a dollar in the donations jar. Weird, huh?"

"Very." I wondered what had offended Davis enough that

he'd had the gumption to leave abruptly. Maybe he was just too emotional because of his sorrow over Lizzie's death. Just seemed odd.

"But on the up side, we raised almost two-hundred-fifty dollars tonight, and Max had a full house, too."

My face must have shifted when Max's name came up because Mart said, "Do we need to talk about Max?"

I shook my head. "No, there will be time for me to think about Max later. Just now, though, I want to be alone, to think about my life and what I want." I had come to that conclusion on the ride home. There was definitely something about Max, but I was smart enough to know that anything or anyone worth pursuing – I couldn't believe I was actually thinking of pursuing Max someday, but I was – was worth waiting to consider when I wasn't on the rebound. "But I am glad he had a full house. Good for him."

"Good for your mom's fundraiser, too. It was a fundraising night. Fifteen percent of all the sales from tonight are going to DNRN."

"Max Davies gave up fifteen percent of his profits?" I was incredulous, not just because my opinion of Max was only beginning to change but because I knew what that kind of donation could cost a small business.

"Not fifteen percent of his profits, Harvey. Fifteen percent of his gross. He probably went into the red tonight." Mart's face was serious. "But he was thrilled. I don't know that I'd ever seen him happier."

I stared at her for a minute and then swallowed hard. I wasn't arrogant enough to think that Max had done this kind thing to attract my attention, but it had . . . and I was definitely paying attention. Not taking action, but paying attention.

Mart patted my knee. "I thought you'd like to know that," she said, and then clicked play.

. . .

THE NEXT MORNING, I woke up the kind of tired that can only come after sadness. I was weary somewhere deep inside, even as my body felt rested, lighter even. I knew I'd done the right thing with Daniel, but it was still hard and sad.

Taco improved things immensely though. It was pretty fun to wake up to a basset hound nose against my neck . . . and then watch him bound across the frost-covered backyard to do his business. Mayhem was too precious to get her paws wet, so she peed just as close to the back door as she could, then scuttled back to the fire. Taco, however, took his time and came back only as the bacon Mart was cooking came off the griddle.

We all ate our bacon and then donned our coats and headed toward the store. Lizzie's funeral was at ten, and I wanted to be there. So Mart and I were going to do the opening of the shop and then, at his own gracious offer, leave Marcus and Rocky in charge, yet again, while we went to the services. It only felt right that I be there, given that I'd found her body and that I'd talked with her mom, but it also felt strange because I hadn't known her at all. Not when she was alive. I did feel like I had a sense of her now, given all the research and conversations we'd had. But still, it felt weird to not go and to go, too. It was a day of paradoxical emotions.

When we walked in and Max gestured for us to join him just behind Mrs. Leicht. I cringed. It felt intrusive, too much presence given the circumstances, but he was so adamant that Mart and I shared a glance and then headed that way. Mart took a step back to let me sit next to Max, and I rolled my eyes at her before sliding into the pew quickly. "Why are we sitting so close?" I whispered.

Max pointed toward Mrs. Leicht. "Her request."

I studied the purple tips on Mrs. Leicht's hair and pondered that information. Maybe we were the only people she knew here, or maybe she knew we were, in some ways, the only people Lizzie knew here. And that thought led me to another, which I whispered to Max, "Why is the funeral being held here?"

Max took a small notebook out of his pocket and began to write. Once again, I was given pause by his thoughtfulness. It was definitely better to write than to whisper in a quiet church before a person was laid to rest.

When he finished, he passed the notebook over to me, and I read. "I asked the same thing. I was pulling together a memorial when we didn't know anything about Lizzie's family, of course, but when Mrs. Leicht came, I had intended to help with arranging for the care of Lizzie's body here and with transportation back to Boston. But her mom and I talked, she said she wanted ~~Lizzie~~ Cassandra to be buried here."

I studied the note a minute and then, after passing it to Mart, looked at Max and gave him my most intentionally puzzled face. He shrugged and motioned for his notebook, but before we could continue our pantomimed and scribbled conversation, the minister came to the pulpit. She began by reading a passage from the Bible. "God is love. When we take up permanent residence in a life of love, we live in God and God lives in us. This way, love has the run of the house, becomes at home and mature in us." It was a beautiful verse, a reminder of what I believed about God and people . . . even though I didn't go to church often because I found it painful to see when love wasn't central there.

Here, in this space, though, when we were honoring the life of someone who, by all accounts, lived a life of love for her customers especially, it felt perfect, like God's self was there, loving us all.

The rest of the service was equally beautiful, and I left the church feeling more at peace, more settled than I had in days. The pastor hadn't known Lizzie, obviously, but she had spoken of the woman with such tenderness that it made me remember that we don't have to know someone to love them, love them well even.

Outside, we saw Tuck and Lu, and instinctively, all of us headed that way. Max and I had suspended our passing of notes, so we still hadn't landed on a reason that Mrs. Leicht had wanted the funeral here.

Mrs. Leicht was standing there, thanking each person who had come. We'd slipped out the side door to avoid the crowd, but I was a little sad to not have let her see us there. I thought about asking her why she wanted her daughter to be buried here but decided it wasn't the time.

As I turned back to my friends, Tuck said, "Oh, I don't know if I can handle this today."

I turned to follow his gaze and saw Davis wheeling toward us.

"You managed to stay for the funeral?" Max asked as he shook Davis's hand.

"I did." He glanced around our small circle. "Figured it was the least I could do. Pay my respects and all."

He sounded sincere, and he certainly looked like he was grieving. Dark circles under his eyes, a pale pallor to his pinkish skin. But I was still a little uneasy about him, about the way he had worked it out to be here when he had been so clear that he couldn't just a couple of days before.

I didn't have much time to ponder through my discomfort though because, just then, Effie walked up. "Hi Harvey. I thought I might see you here." Her eyes scanned the faces around me, resting for an extra second on Davis's before moving on.

If I was baffled about how Davis was able to be here for the funeral, I was absolutely stymied by *why* Effie was here at all. "Oh, hi Effie. Um, were you here for the funeral?" I looked around, trying to see if something else might have drawn her. Yard sale maybe. But there wasn't anything.

"I was." Her voice was calm and even. "I read about the murder in the paper and saw that her service was today. Since she was from Boston, too, I figured I could honor her with my presence. Thought maybe there wouldn't be many people there." She looked at the crowd of about thirty-five people still milling in the church. "Guess I didn't need to worry."

Lu said, "It was kind of you to come. Most of the people here came for the same reason. It's sort of an unspoken rule of the small town – make sure everyone knows they are loved, even after they die."

I sighed. She was right. Time and again, I'd seen the people of St. Marin's show up when their neighbors and the visitors to our town needed them. Just a couple of weeks ago, a young couple visiting from Arizona had been in a terrible car accident just outside of town, and both of them wound up in the hospital. The local quilting circle heard about their accident from one of their members who was a volunteer at the information desk there, and they took it upon themselves to meet the couple, find out who they could call, and then sit with them until their family could arrive. Even after the couple's parents had come down, the quilters brought them food every day of their hospital stay.

"Well, I'm glad I'm not the only one," Effie said. "Just wanted to say hello, Harvey. And thanks again for the book recommendations."

She turned to go, but Tuck stopped her with a light touch on the arm. "Actually, we were all about to go get some lunch. Would you like to join us?" He looked from Effie to Davis.

Mart, Max, and I exchanged glances but said nothing. Tuck did few things spontaneously. He was a methodical man, so if he wanted lunch with two almost strangers, we were going to get lunch.

"I'll pull the truck around," Lu said, and I saw Davis's eyes go wide.

"She drives a food truck. Correction THE BEST food truck," I said. "Her tacos are amazing." For a split second, I felt a pang since Daniel and I had often shared Lu's tacos for lunch, but then, I pushed my mind and heart back to the present moment and tried to figure out Tuck's purpose as we moved toward the church's side lot, where Lu often set up to catch traffic to and from the nearby high school.

Inside, the church members would have set up a lunch for Mrs. Leicht and any guests who wanted to attend, and I could see that a lot of the folks who had come out for the funeral were headed in the side door for the meal. We didn't need to be there, especially if not going might mean we got some more clarity on Lizzie's murder. That seemed the only reason Tuck might have made his suggestion.

A large picnic table sat under trees at the back of the lot by the playground, and we all huddled close on them, trying to conserve body heat. Davis rolled to the end of the table and locked in his chair. He couldn't rub arms or legs with the rest of us, and I worried he might be very cold. But then he pulled a wool blanket out of a backpack on the back of his chair and tucked it around his legs. I wished I'd thought to do the same.

Effie sat opposite me, and Mart squeezed in beside me almost pushing Max out of the way to do so. I appreciated her efforts, although a tiny part of me was sad, too. Again, I forced my mind back to the topic at hand and focused. Why, exactly, did Tuck want Effie and Davis to stay for lunch?

As he brought over trays of the food Lu had premade for her lunch crowd, I got my answer. He set down a platter of enchiladas covered in queso and cheddar and said, "Davis, do you know, Effie? I mean, I know Boston is a big city, but maybe since you own such a popular restaurant?"

Davis turned to Effie on his right and said, "You're from Boston." He held out a hand. "Nice to meet you."

For a split second, I saw a wave of something – concern, fear

– pass over Effie's face, but then she put out her hand and said, "Yep. Mattapan born and raised." Her accent got thick as she said the name, I assumed, of her neighborhood.

"Dorchester," Davis replied, and they began a conversation about the communities of Boston that left me both hungry to visit again and totally lost.

So I made myself content with two chicken tacos and a heaping pile of the chips Lu fried fresh every morning and listened. By the time the two Bostoners had covered their family histories, they seemed like old friends, and one look at Tuck told me that this was exactly what he had been hoping would happen.

And then, as if on cue, he said, "So I have a question for both of you. Is it expensive to have a funeral in Boston?"

Both Davis and Effie looked at the sheriff with befuddlement, but finally, Effie spoke. "I mean, Boston is definitely more expensive than here. Just like any city. But funerals aren't particularly expensive." She paused and studied Tuck's face. "Why do you ask?"

He took a big bite of enchilada and took his time chewing and swallowing before answering. I recognized his quintessential technique for looking casual while he bought time to think. He wiped his mouth with a napkin and said, "Oh, I was just curious because I'd have thought Lizzie's, I mean, Cassandra's mom would have taken her home to be buried."

Effie nodded and studied Tuck's face a minute more. "Maybe this was just easier. Maybe they don't have a lot of family up there."

Tuck shrugged and took another monstrous bite of food, waiting, I knew, for more conversation that arose.

"I guess that's possible," Max added, "but it still seems odd. I mean, she's being buried here, right?" He pointed over toward the cemetery beside the church.

I actually didn't know the answer to that question. There

hadn't been an invitation to the cemetery, so it was possible there was going to be a private burial. But it was also possible the burial wasn't taking place here at all. I looked over at Tuck, and he gave me one of *those* stares that meant, "Play along, Harvey."

"I expect it's going to be a private burial." I glanced over to the cemetery and was glad to see that the local funeral home had put up one of their canopies in the back corner by the large oaks. "Looks like they're getting set up now." A few men in suits were gathered, and as we watched, I saw them walk into the church and then return with Lizzie's casket, which they placed on a steel frame set over an open grave.

"Looks like it," Davis said, and I could hear some taint of something in his voice, something that sounded a lot like anger. "I wonder if I could attend."

"I doubt it," Mart said. "I guess you could crash, but if the congregation wasn't invited during the service, it probably means Mrs. Leicht prefers to be alone."

Davis gave a curt nod and then glanced back at the funeral home tent. Effie studied him, then the grave, then him again before she caught me watching her and dropped her eyes. "It does seem strange," she said, "to have her buried here, but I expect she has her reasons." Effie shrugged and finished the last bite of her enchilada. Then she wiped her mouth and stood. "Thank you for inviting me for lunch. I think I'm going to take in that maritime museum, if it's worth it."

"Definitely worth it," Mart said as she stood. "Let me walk you over and introduce you to our friend Lucas, the director. Maybe he'll have time to give you a special tour."

Effie's face lit up. "Oh, I'd love that. I'm a bit of a military history buff, naval stuff mostly." She waved, and Mart gave me a sly wink as she walked away. She was up to something.

I began gathering the trash and carrying it to the trash can Lu had set out by the truck, and when I turned back to the table, Davis was gone, wheeling his way toward the cemetery. So much for manners, I thought, and started to head toward him to ask that he please respect Mrs. Leicht's wishes when Tuck caught my eye and shook his head just slightly.

I stared at him a minute, and he gave me "the look" again. So I finished cleaning up and then went to Lu's window. "This was all a big set-up wasn't it?" I said quietly.

She smiled. "Hey, you got your tacos out of it." She slid a plate with her amazing flan on it in my direction. "A little thanks for catching on so quickly."

I grinned and took the plate back to the table with the three forks she'd given me, and Tuck, Max, and I devoured the delicious pudding in seconds flat. Then, after a quick look around to be sure we were alone, I said, "What in the world is going on, Tuck?"

He smirked at me and then winked at Max, who surprisingly was also grinning like the Cheshire Cat. "Wait, am I the only one not in on this?"

A furrow appeared on Max's brow as he saw my expression. "Oh no, we've hurt your feelings. He reached across and patted my hand. "I'm so sorry."

I braced myself for some snide comment, some dismissive remark. But none came. He just squeezed my finger one more time and then looked to Tuck.

"I know, Harvey. It was an unkind thing to do to a friend, but we needed you to not know what was happening because—" he faltered for a minute.

"Because I don't have a poker face and have a really hard time keeping a secret." My shoulders dropped, and I knew he was right. It still stung that my friends hadn't trusted me with whatever they were planning, but I knew that my hurt feelings were incidental if this was about finding a murderer. "Okay, we can address that later, but can you tell me what's up now?"

Tuck licked the back of his spoon and then looked at me.

"Lizzie is not being buried here. That was all a ruse. I asked Mrs. Leicht if we could stage a funeral here just to see who might turn up, and it worked. All of our suspects were here."

"All of them? You mean more than just Davis and Effie?" I stared at my friend and tried to think like an investigator, and like that, a light went off. "And Mrs. Leicht! You got her to play along so you could keep her close."

A single finger to the side of Tuck's nose signaled I was right. "It gave me a bit more time to look into things if everyone stayed in town, and I got to see two of our suspects interact up close and personal."

Max smiled and looked at me. "Lunch was part of the plan, too," he said.

"And this?" I gestured over to where Mrs. Leicht and Davis were disagreeing, in even louder and louder tones, near the fresh grave.

"Part of it, too," Tuck said as he stood, "although it is getting heated. I told her to ask him to leave if he came over, but I wasn't expecting a fight." Tuck jogged toward the altercation, and at the same moment he reached the two people, Mrs. Leicht pulled back her arm and got ready to throw a punch.

Fortunately, Tuck held her back, and Davis – face red and sweaty – moved back, too. We'd almost had a fist-fight in a church cemetery. I leaned over to Max, who had joined me at standing by the edge of the graveyard. "I take it that wasn't part of the plan."

He shook his head but then smiled just a little, and I found myself smiling too.

Davis got into a van and peeled out of the parking lot a few moments later, and after Tuck had given us a subtle nod, Max and I departed, too, with a wave of thanks to Lu. We walked back to Main Street in silence, and while I felt like I should say something, I couldn't figure out what that something should be. So I didn't say anything, and when we parted at the door to his restaurant, I was glad we hadn't. It wasn't time for whatever we wanted or needed to say between us. Might not be for a while yet, and that was okay, too.

Back at the shop, the store was humming, not with the frenzy of yesterday but steadily. Between people coming in to see if we had any remaining tickets – which we didn't – and a steady stream of locals breaking forth into the world after our intense cold snap, we were busy, and I was glad.

While I tidied shelves and filled holes in our window displays, I pondered Lizzie's death, and I kept coming back to her prosthetic arm. Where was it exactly? I'm sure Tuck would have told me if it had been in her apartment somewhere – they'd searched it the day after she died – so where was it? The most obvious answer was that it had been stolen, but as Mrs. Leicht said, it was custom-made for Lizzie. But maybe it was easier to alter/adjust/modify – I didn't know what verb was right – an existing arm than to create a new one.

I knew that was probably the simple truth – a theft to go along with the murder – but something about that didn't feel right, especially since there wasn't any trace of a break-in back at her apartment in Boston and so few people knew she was here. No, something is off with that idea.

I grabbed a huge stack of magazines from the tote in the back of the store and began to organize and refill our rack. Tuck had said the arm had a serial number that was easily traceable, but nothing had come up on a search. So either the person who stole the arm wasn't trying to sell it or have it modified and was laying low for a while, which was plausible, I guess. Or it wasn't stolen, and Lizzie had kept it somewhere.

Again, I found myself backed up against a case of too little information, and without butting in where I wasn't welcome, I didn't have any way of learning more. But not learning more wasn't really feeling like an option at the moment, so I took out my phone, ready to call the B&B where Mrs. Leicht had mentioned she was staying. I needed to get into Lizzie's apartment here in town and look around.

But before I could dial, Mart texted. "You're going to LOVE this," her message said.

I started to text her back, but just then, Tuck came in with Effie close behind him.

"Harvey, can we chat a minute?" The sheriff's voice was light, but his expression was serious. I gave a curt nod, caught Marcus's eye, and saw his thumbs up in return as I led Tuck and Effie to the back room.

"What's up, Tuck? Everything okay." I looked from him to Effie and back again. Effie nodded to the chair and then looked at me, waiting for approval to sit.

"Of course," I said before sitting, too. "This seems serious. Is everything okay?"

Tuck took the third seat at the table and looked at me. "I've just learned that Effie here is with the FBI."

10

"In Boston?" My brain was trying hard to put all the pieces together, and since the only real thing I knew was that Effie was from Boston and knew Galen, my synapses were trying to connect what details I had.

"Yes, actually." She smiled at me. "I haven't actually lied to you."

I felt like that was supposed to be comforting, but when someone says they haven't lied, it implies either that they are lying now or that lying might not be the big concern here. "Okaay," I said slowly.

"I'm investigating a series of suspicious disappearances of people within the disability rights community there. Lizzie wasn't the first." She put her phone on the table and opened what looked like a file of documents. Then, she stopped at an image and handed the phone to me.

"This man went missing three months ago. He is blind." She paused and looked at Tuck, who nodded, before continuing. "He's recently undergone an experimental surgery using prosthetic corneas."

"They can do that," I blurted and then quickly blushed as I

realized I'd missed the larger bit about him being missing. "Sorry. So he's still missing?"

"He is. And so are about five other people who have recently received prosthetic devices, state of the art ones. We're pretty sure there's a connection." She looked at me then as if she was waiting for me to say something.

And boy did I have things to say. All the words wanted to tumble out of my mouth at once, but instead of sharing actually useful information I said, "I feel like I'm in a thriller. Is James Patterson recording this as research?" I pretended to look around for hidden cameras until my eyes landed on Tuck's disapproving expression.

"Agent Li, Harvey has a tendency to turn everything into a plotline when she's nervous." Tuck gave the agent a knowing look and then smirked at me.

"Well, it doesn't help when you call her Agent Li," I said as I rolled my eyes.

"Please, call me Effie. It's easier for everyone and a lot less intense." She smiled, and I felt my nervousness dissipate a little.

"Actually, I'm so glad you told me, because I've been trying to figure out what the prosthetic arm that Mrs. Leicht mentioned has been bugging me so much. I mean, something like that—"

Effie interrupted. "Mrs. Leicht told you about Lizzie's arm?"

The tone of her voice slowed me way down, and I studied her face for a moment. "Yeah, she mentioned that it was missing and that it seemed odd that Lizzie, I mean Cassandra, hadn't brought it here with her." I sat back in my chair and let my mind slide over the questions I'd had. "But she said it wasn't in Lizzie's apartment, and I couldn't imagine Lizzie leaving behind something so expensive. So it just got me thinking, I guess." I didn't have anything concrete to share about my wild imaginations that Lizzie might have stashed the arm somewhere, so I stopped talking.

"Well, I'd really like to talk this through with both of you," Effie said. "It seems like you've got a nose for the kind of lateral thinking that investigations require, Harvey."

Tuck tried to cover up his groan with a cough. "Um, go ahead, Agent Li." His voice was casual, but he was giving me the "You aren't getting in the middle of this" death stare.

"Well, it's probably important for you to know that Cassandra did not use her prosthetic arm often. In fact, from what we've gathered, she only used it once, the first day she got it. After that, she never put it on."

"Did it hurt or something? Or didn't it work well?" I asked.

"Actually, it worked just fine, at least that's what her colleagues said, and no one heard her complain about discomfort." Effie leaned back and rested one forearm on the chair back behind her. "She'd had extensive training on how to use the arm and it had been fit at the company where it was made. No, this seems to be more about Cassandra's preferences."

Tuck leaned into the table further. "She didn't want to wear the prosthetic? Then why have it made?"

That question was a much more delicate and appropriate one than what I had wanted to ask. I had been about to say, "Why wouldn't she want her arm back?" which with a second of pause, I realized was quite the ableist thing to say. To presume that Lizzie, or anyone with a disability, wanted to get rid of that disability implies that there is something defective about that person. That's what I'd learned in all my reading about disability rights.

"That's what we don't know. I've been working this case for about nine months now, and it seems like a lot of people pressure their loved ones who might use assistive devices to get them, even if the person doesn't want to." She ran her fingers through her black hair. "It takes a lot of will power to stand up to that kind of pressure."

"Especially if it might go on for the rest of your life," I said with a shake of my head. "I probably would have caved, too. I can't even take the peer pressure over eating at a restaurant I don't really like much less a fundamental element about how I live my life."

I thought of the way Stephen had recently coerced me into going out for sushi by saying I'd probably like nori and could just get the rolls with rice. I had been skeptical and suggested a fusion place where I could get other things. But he really wanted this particular sushi restaurant, so I went along and learned quickly that my aversion to seafood needs to broaden to include anything that lives in water, especially nori.

"And even more especially if that someone is your mother," Effie added with a pointed look at me from the corner of her eye.

I sighed. "Well, that explains why Mrs. Leicht was so curious about it, I guess." I remembered Lizzie's mom's face when she'd been telling me. I'd taken that gleam in her eye as sadness, but maybe there had been a little anger there, too.

Tuck cleared his throat. "That's the thing. We don't understand Mrs. Leicht's motivations. Why is she here? Is she trying to play up the grieving mother bit, or is this something else?"

I thought about my conversations with Mrs. Leicht and had to admit she had been a little cold. Well, a lot cold. But my own mother wasn't the warm and fuzzy type, so it hadn't really put me off. Maybe I'd missed something. Could Mrs. Leicht really have killed her own daughter? "So you think she made up that whole thing about hearing the hotel clerks talking just to throw us off?"

Effie shrugged as she paced around the room. "Maybe." She stopped at the large whiteboard I had tucked into the corner, a leftover part of one of my most misguided attempts to "assist" in an investigation, and said, "Mind if I use this?

I shrugged, and she pulled it out and grabbed the blue marker still on the tray below it. "We know that all the missing people, including Cassandra, had assistive devices that were designed to accommodate their disability in some way. But we also know that none of these people chose to use their devices on a regular basis." She wrote "Had them/hated them" on the board.

"How many people are we talking about here?" I asked.

"Twelve," Tuck said as he turned his chair to see the white board more fully. "Didn't you say twelve over the last fifteen months?"

"That's right. All of them are in the Boston area. All of them received the most technologically advanced devices out there." She made more notes on the board.

I stretched and got my brain in gear again. "Did all of them have family or friends who pressured them to use the devices?"

"Oh, that's a good question. Let me think." Effie put the pen in her mouth and stared off into the middle distance. "Cassandra's mom told her she needed it to look "whole and complete" again."

"Oof," I said as Effie continued.

"This man's sister said he couldn't really be a good farmer unless he could run all the equipment without devices. 'Real men didn't need their hands to do what their feet should.'" She raised her eyebrows and looked at Tuck and I. "That's an exact quote."

One by one, Effie ticked off the people who were missing, and a couple of moments later she said, "Yep, everyone had gotten considerable pressure to use their devices. Now that's an angle I'd missed until now. Thanks, Harvey."

I blushed and felt my ego grow two sizes bigger, like the Grinch's heart, and wondered how Tuck would keep me in check now. The glare he shot my way was my answer.

"But you don't know if any of these other people were murdered, right?" Tuck's question brought me out of my own pride with a thud.

"No, we haven't found any other reports of murders that match our missing people. Doesn't mean they're not there, but probably not. As soon as your report hit the online records, our team flagged it because of the description. That is one thing – people with a physical disability often stand out." She sat back down and stared at the whiteboard.

I followed her gaze and studied her notes for a moment. "So we really only think we have one murder, right? Since, as you said, your team would have probably already flagged other murders of disabled people?

"That's what I'm thinking," Effie said. "I just don't know what that means."

Tuck spoke softly. "Seems to me that all the disappearances are connected, even Cassandra's. But something went wrong here. Maybe someone found her, and they couldn't find everyone else."

I nodded. That seemed right, somehow, but not completely so. I was loath to correct the sheriff, but they'd let me sit in, so I figured I had some room to speak. "Right, but the other people haven't been found, even by the FBI. So either they're really good at hiding, which could be the case, or once they were gone, the person who killed Lizzie didn't care enough to track them down."

"Someone cared about Cassandra, though, wanted to find her," Tuck continued my train of thought. "Wanted to find her so that they could kill her?"

"Maybe," Effie said, "or maybe they wanted to find her and bring her back. Maybe the thing that's different is that the killer didn't actually want Cassandra to disappear. Maybe they wanted her to come back, and when she wouldn't . . ."

We let the rest of her sentence hang in the air.

Finally, Tuck said, "We're looking for the person who wanted to find Cassandra badly enough to hunt her down."

Effie nodded, and I felt my stomach sink. That someone had found her . . . and killed her

I LEFT Tuck and Effie talking law enforcement strategy in the breakroom and headed back out on the floor. I had appreciated the chance to brainstorm with them, and I was glad I'd gotten to share what I did know. But the whole idea of someone tracking Lizzie – I really needed to start calling her Cassandra – down and, for whatever reason, killing her, was bringing up memories I tried not to engage if I could.

Back in high school, this guy had stalked me. In comparison to the way they depicted stalking on TV – whole rooms full of pictures with the eyes blacked out and stuff – my situation had been mild. But it was still terrifying to have him show up outside my bedroom window in the middle of the night, and when he and his girlfriend had appeared at my dorm one night only so he could try to follow me to my room while she sat in the lounge, I began to get really scared. Finally, my mom had answered the phone when he called one night and told him that if he ever contacted me again, she'd have him arrested. And that had slowed him down . . . until social media, but by then, I could block him, and block him I did.

As I wandered the store floor and reshelved books, I kept thinking about Lizzie, about why she had run. Maybe it had been a part of this whole weirdness about using prosthetics or not, but I didn't think that was the whole story. It felt like she was afraid, and she'd run . . . for her life, maybe.

At five, I sent Marcus home with my deep gratitude for covering for me so much over the past few days. "Take tomorrow off. You, too, Rocky. I'll cover the cafe," I said as they walked to the door together. "I've got the shop and the cafe tonight. It's going to be slow."

The crisp cold had returned as the sun had moved closer to

setting, and with sunset coming at four thirty, the streets would be pretty empty in our quiet town. I'd probably get a couple of college kids from Salisbury, and maybe a local or two out for date night while the kids were with a sitter. Nothing I couldn't handle on my own. "You kids have fun," I said with full-on sarcasm as they rolled their eyes and walked to Rocky's car. They were so cute.

I was right. The night was quiet. Made a few sales. Fumbled my way through a few espressos. Sold the rest of the Rice Krispies treats, mostly to myself. And at seven, I turned off the Open sign, set the alarm, and let Mayhem and Taco lead me whatever direction they wanted for our walk home. Mart and I had agreed to a *Friends* marathon starting at eight with a huge extra cheese pizza that Symeon was going to make for us, so I had a little time to wander in the cool air.

The dogs headed me north, and at first, I thought we'd be heading straight home. But instead, they took me down some of the quiet residential streets in town. I loved these homes with the golden glow of lamps coming from living rooms, where some couples sat reading or families were curled up in front of televisions. One woman about my age stood in the middle of her living room and matched about three hundred pairs of white socks. It was fascinating, and I was glad the dogs' noses took me by again. So many white socks.

Finally, after wandering long enough that I thought the neighbors might think we were casing their houses, I gave the dogs the cue – "Home, boys" – and they began to point their sniffers in the direction of our house. We were just making the penultimate turn toward our house when I noticed two people talking by a parked car. Normally, I wouldn't have paid much attention – well, I would have paid attention but only in a nosy way, not a suspicious one – but I saw one of the people had spiky hair, and I saw a gleam off of what looked to be wheelchair wheels.

Quickly, I steered the dogs that way and began a random conversation with them to act as if I was totally distracted. "Any scent of squirrels yet guys? Maybe spring will come soon?" "Sasquatch been by lately. He just lives up the street you know." I rambled my way along the block trying to look entirely interested in what the dogs were doing until I came to the car where I swore Mrs. Leicht and Davis had been talking. But when I looked up, they were gone.

I didn't want to stand still and look around. That would be far too suspicious, so I just kept talking to the pups and resumed the walk toward home. I had a moment's hesitation about going there because I remembered some story from junior high about how you should never lead the person following you to your house, but I quickly dismissed that concern for two reasons. First, I didn't think I was being followed. Secondly, in a town as small as St. Marin's, if someone wanted to know where you lived, they could just ask, well, anyone.

Still, I was disconcerted for the rest of the walk and only kept my pace even because I knew – as clueless as they seemed – that these two ridiculous dogs would protect me if it came to it. They'd done it before.

When we got home, though, I left the outside lights on, bolted the door behind me, and spent the first few minutes making sure the back door and windows were locked.

As I finished my security check, Mart shook her head, handed me a glass of wine, and pointed to the plate of cheese and crackers and the bowl of popcorn before she said, "You're in danger again, aren't you?"

I sighed.

"Better fill me in," she said. "But before you do, let's be clear about something. I get to be Rachel for putting up with your nosiness, Chandler."

I huffed, but she was right. I was totally Bing-ing this up.

. . .

THE NEXT MORNING by unspoken agreement, Mart and I decided not to talk about Lizzie. I think we both knew we were just spinning our wheels trying to figure anything out in the absence of some crucial information we just didn't have, and so instead, we spent our chatter over breakfast and on the walk into the shop talking about how the "young people" were watching *Friends* these days but seemed to be doing so ironically, like our young adulthood was something to be mocked, not treasured.

By the time, we reached the store, both of us were acting like we needed walkers and had lost all our teeth while saying things like, "Get off my lawn, you pesky kids" and lamenting the sad return of high-waisted jeans. "They used to be 'Mom-jeans'," Mart moaned as I unlocked the door, "and now they're trendy."

"These young whippersnappers have no appreciation of taste," I said as I shook my fist before flipping on the lights and laughing as Mart hobbled over to the cafe on her imaginary cane. There was a reason that woman was my best friend, and this schtick here in our middle age was a good part of that reason.

I was still smiling as I logged into the register and walked the floor to take a quick scan of our status. The shelves looked full and neat, and something in my bones was telling me it was going to be a good day. I always liked Sundays in the shop. Mostly, they were quiet, especially in the morning when most of St. Marin's was at church, and I liked having time to talk to every customer that came in.

The first customer in was a white guy who looked to be in his early thirties. Mutton-chop sideburns and really cute booties had me thinking of Noel from *The Great British Baking Show*, but I didn't mention that comparison since he, it turned out, was looking for some help picking out a romance novel for his grandmother. "She reads like the things like she's eating potato chips," he said, "so I try to take one each time I visit."

I smiled. Romance readers were voracious, and while I didn't read many titles, I did try to stay on top of the latest trends so I could recommend well. "What kind of books is she into? I mean, I know she likes romance," I added when he raised an eyebrow. "But does she want sex or no sex?"

To his credit, the man blushed, and I said quickly, "Okay, so sweet romance. Humor or history?"

"Oh, Gran is really funny, so humor."

"Awesome. I think I'd like to meet your gran," I said as I pulled Emma St. Clair's *Falling for Your Best Friend's Twin* from the shelf. "This one should do the trick. It's new and had me laughing out loud several times. Plus, it's a sweet story. And I think she'll like the heroine because she's a little out of the mainstream." I gave his booties a knowing look, and the man grinned.

"Perfect," he said as we walked to the register.

I was feeling a little smug that I'd been able to make a romance sale based on a book I'd actually read in that section when Davis rolled in the door. My mood soured at just the sight of him, and I wasn't sure why. We'd gotten off on the wrong foot, of course, but he'd apologized and been great since. But that whole crashing the burial thing just bugged me, as did his sudden ability to hang around for the service. Something just felt off.

Still, I put on a big smile and greeted him warmly with a handshake. "What can I do for you, Davis? Here to pick up some reading?" I gestured around the store.

"Actually, now that you mention it, maybe. Audio books?"

I didn't carry a huge audio collection because they were so expensive to buy, and most people got theirs through the library or a subscription service. But I did have a few. "What kind of reading do you like?"

He stared at me for a minute like I'd just asked him what his favorite flavor of blue was. But then said, "Oh, something fast-paced if you have it."

I ran my fingers along the clamshell cases until I came to *Brother Odd* by Dean Koontz and took it off the shelf. "You okay with a little supernatural stuff?"

He shrugged, and I placed the book in his hands. "This one will serve you well. Fast-paced and intriguing. Plus, if you like, there's a whole series."

"Sounds good," he said and raised the book up. "I'll take it." He wheeled his chair toward the register. "I also wanted to ask a favor."

I took as deep a breath as subtlety would allow and said, "Happy to help if I can."

"I'm heading back to Boston today. Could you let the sheriff know? He has my number, and I'm available to answer questions anytime. But I really need to get back to my business."

"Okay, I'll tell him," I said as I rang up his book and swiped his card. "But it might be a good idea for you to give him a call at the station, you know, so it's official." I really didn't like to imagine Tuck's face when I told him one of his prime suspects had left town and that I'd known. "Actually, let me just call him now, okay?"

I picked up my phone and had just tapped Tuck's name in my contacts when Davis rolled out the door with a wave. I groaned as the call connected, and Tuck answered.

"I tried, Tuck."

I could hear his sigh through the phone. "What happened?"

At least I couldn't see his expression since I told him on the phone, but given the icy tone to his voice, his disapproval came through loud and clear.

"What did you want me to do? Tackle him? Put a boot on his

wheelchair? Stand in front of him like I would a toddler heading for the street until you could get here?" I knew the sheriff was frustrated, but seriously, I'm not supposed to help with things until I am. Talk about mixed signals.

"Any of those options would have worked," he said and let out a long whistle. "But it's okay. I know his car and plates. I'll put out the word to the Boston PD and ask them to keep an eye out. They'll let me know if he shows up anywhere he shouldn't."

I imagined police officers staking out his house, lots of coffee and sandwiches from one of those corner delis, and then I checked myself. *Not TV, Harvey. Not TV.* "Good idea."

"I'll let Effie know, too." I could hear the clicks of Tuck's keyboard. "Thanks." Then he hung up. At least he didn't sound mad anymore.

11

A bit later that morning, I puttered over to Mart in the cafe and got my morning latte as I told her about what had just happened. "People need to deliver their own messages," she said.

"Tell me about it." One woman was sitting in the window of the cafe with a stack of comic books and a cup of coffee. She was reading intently while she twisted a dreadlock around her finger. I watched her for a moment and felt my frustration fade. She was doing just what I loved for people to do – read in my store – and I couldn't stay in a bad mood when that was happening.

The bell over the door rang, and I made my way back to the books as a trio of teenage girls headed to the YA section and started laughing and swapping favorite scenes from Leigh Bardugo's *Shadow and Bone.* Apparently, one of the girls – a blonde with a brilliant pink streak in her hair – hadn't finished the trilogy yet, and there was much gasping and horror over this fact from the other two, a short Asian girl with plaid pants and suspenders and a brunette with the whitest skin I had ever seen. I resisted asking if she liked vampire fiction, though, because she probably did, and she probably wouldn't get my joke.

They were deep into a good browse and didn't need me, so I went back to the front of the store and scanned the displays. Everything looked amazing, and we'd had steady sales of the titles Marcus had chosen. I knew some of that was just the natural result of putting a book where people could find it. Some folks were bound to be interested in any title, but I knew most of those titles had sold because of the event. People liked to be prepared for new things, and while the turnout for tickets to our roller rink night was impressive, I also knew that many a St. Mariner was learning all they could about disability rights so as not to make a fool of themselves.

I was doing the same thing when I pulled a copy of *Being Heumann* down and took it back to the counter to read. It was one of the prerogatives of a bookstore owner to be able to read on the job. That was a perk in and of itself, but without fail, I was always asked what I was reading when I had a book open. More often than not, the conversation that rose up out of my answer resulted in a sale of that book, sometimes the very copy I'd been reading. I was about one-third of the way through a dozen books that I'd sold right out of my own hands, and I didn't hate that.

Today, I didn't sell the book away from myself, but I did answer a lot of questions about it as well as hand out a fair number of pamphlets about the National Disability Rights Network. And because the shop was slow, I disappeared into Heumann's story and found myself both angry and motivated to do more to make the world more accessible for people.

First, I knew I needed to change some things in the store. So when I needed to let my eyes rest a bit, I took a walk around the shop and made a few decisions. I had put in a wheelchair accessible bathroom when I renovated the old gas station building, but it had never occurred to me that someone in a wheelchair or using a walker or canes might struggle with the front door of the shop because it was heavy and not on a hydraulic arm. I was going to get that arm put in asap so that the door didn't slam shut quickly on someone.

I also hadn't ever thought about putting braille signs up, but now I decided that I'd label the book sections as well as each door clearly so that a blind person could navigate the store more easily. Plus, I needed to beef up the audio section a bit to make my offerings for the visually impaired more robust.

Finally, I printed up a bold, clear sign that said, "All animals welcome, especially service animals. Please let us know if your animal needs us to confine our own dogs when you visit," and looked up how to have this sign printed in braille for those with guide dogs.

I felt a little ashamed that I hadn't thought of these things sooner, but I wasn't about to let that shame stop me from doing them now.

Those decisions plus the steady stream of customers that started filing in as churches let out had me feeling downright gleeful by early afternoon. Books were selling. People were reading. Children were petting Taco and Mayhem and asking if they could take them home. It was a good day.

Then, Mrs. Leicht came in, and the minute I saw her face, I knew my blissful Sunday was about to take a turn into shadow. "Hello, Mrs. Leicht," I said as she stalked over to the counter. "Anything I can help you with?"

She saw the book I was reading and scoffed. She actually made a sound that sounded like "scoff." "Garbage," she spat.

"Oh, I think it's really good. You read it, though, and didn't like it?" Not all books were for all people, so I tried to keep that in mind in all discussions about books people really detest.

"No, I didn't read that. It's nonsense. All this fighting for rights." She rolled her eyes, and I wondered if she'd complete the trifecta of disdain with the raising of a certain finger, but I was spared that display when she changed the subject. "I saw you at the funeral yesterday. You bought it, huh?"

I tried to recover from the whiplash of those five sentences by shaking my head slightly. Typically, "I saw you at my daughter's funeral" is followed by some obligatory kind word like "Thank you for coming" or "It was kind of you to be there." Not a query about whether it felt sufficiently morose as to be believable.

I knew that the fake burial and such had been Tuck's idea, and I understood why he did it and why Mrs. Leicht agreed. But I didn't get why she'd be reveling in that deception, especially when the service had been, in fact, quite moving for me and for others, I expected. "It was a lovely service, even if it was a bit of a performance," I said with a small hope that maybe this brashness was a false front for grief.

"That Davis fellow definitely bought it. Came over to the burial like he was going to put himself in the ground with Cassandra. Saw that Oriental lady, too, and she looked like she was believing my acting job, too. Maybe I should go into TV."

I knew she was kidding, at least mostly, but I didn't know what to say. So instead, I pondered how she could live this long in a major city and not know that it was rude to call a person "Oriental." Or maybe she did know and didn't care. That was probably more like it. "Yes, Davis was very upset yesterday, and I don't think Effie knew your daughter personally. But she's from Boston, and when she heard, she wanted—"

Mrs. Leicht cut me off. "Yeah, she wanted to pay her respects. The real funeral will be very small on Thursday up in Boston. Just me and Cassandra's cousins. Then, we'll have all this behind us." Her voice broke just a little, and I felt all the animosity that had been building in me dissipate a little. She was still a grieving mother.

"I'm glad you get to take Cassandra home," I said and put my hand on her arm. "It'll be good that you can have her close."

She met my eyes and said, "It will. But I can't get a head-stone yet. Promised that sheriff of yours that I wouldn't even have a burial service in case someone was watching." She sighed. "But at least she'll be there."

I squeezed her arm. "That will be good, and hopefully soon you can visit her."

"Visit her? I'm not going to some cemetery to see a body. Nope. That's just not me." All tenderness that had crept into the room disappeared like smoke.

"Oh, I see. I just thought . . ." I didn't even finish the thought. Clearly having Lizzie's, Cassandra's body back home in Boston was more of a proprietary gesture than an emotional one, and it wasn't worth my energy or emotion to try to understand or change that. So, I didn't. It didn't feel worth it to try to even think through a perception that said a woman's body needed to be one hundred percent "restored" to be its best but that this same body wasn't a worthy place to remember the woman to whom it belonged. I took a long, deep breath.

"Was there something I could do for you, Mrs. Leicht?" I really wanted this conversation to be done, so anything I could do to move us along was on the table. I even thought about putting my hand on her elbow and moving her slowly toward the door, but she spread her legs and settled her hips into the ground like she was about to do a wicked triangle pose in an impromptu yoga session. I tried to make the second deep breath I needed subtle.

"Actually, yes. I wanted to ask you about the basset hound. Is he for sale?"

I must have stared at her for thirty seconds before I got my mouth working. "No, no he's not." I wanted to leave it at that, but my curiosity wouldn't let me. "Why do you ask?"

"Well, he's in the window with that other mutt. I thought maybe you were adopting out dogs or running a side business selling pure-breeds." She pointed toward the front window where Mayhem and Taco were sprawled like they were recovering from a doggie ultra-marathon.

I smiled until I looked back at Mrs. Leicht's face and realized she was expecting me to say more. "Um, no, those are my dogs. Taco is the Basset Hound, and Mayhem is the Black Mouth Cur. Neither is for sale." I stopped myself before I said something about how Mayhem was not a mutt but a very special rescue who gave me companionship and loyalty, two things her daughter might have appreciated. A mutt, my butt.

Mrs. Leicht looked only mildly disappointed, which told me all I needed to know about her as a potential dog owner, but fortunately, I was saved from further conversation along this line by the arrival of Cate, Lucas, and Sasquatch, their Scottish Terrier, who bounded into the front window with his buddies and immediately took their cue for body position. It looked like either a giant sleep over or like three dogs had collapsed together. I, for one, found it adorable.

"He's not for sale either," I said wryly to Mrs. Leicht, intending the statement as a light joke, but she just sighed and headed toward the front door.

"I'll be around until Tuesday when I'm riding back up with Cassandra," she said. "Maybe I'll make it to that roller rink thing you're having. Sounds like fun."

I didn't have the energy to tell her we were sold out or to point out that if she thought her daughter wasn't "whole" without her arm, an event for a disability rights organization might not be a great place for her. I just smiled and waved as she left.

CATE and Lucas tracked Mrs. Leicht as she swung the front door open with a flourish before they turned to me and said, "Well, what was that all about?"

"Apparently, Mrs. Leicht won't be visiting her daughter's grave, and she wants to buy Taco."

Cate's mouth opened slightly with shock before she said, "Clearly, we need to sit down and get the whole story."

The store was quiet, so we took a table in the cafe near my register in case I needed to tend to customers. Then, I gave them the whole day's run down.

They, too, thought Davis's request was just outright weird and Mrs. Leicht's attitude downright cold, and I took comfort that my reactions weren't off-base. Then, I said, "What brings you in?"

"Well, your mom asked me to make cupcakes for Wednesday, but she told me to just 'be creative,'" Lucas said.

I groaned because I knew that was a trap that Lucas could probably not avoid. My mother was a perfectionist, so while she really, really wanted to allow people creative freedom, it was always better for everyone if she just said what she wanted. Sadly, she was also perfectionistic about her self-image, and her ideal self-image didn't impose itself on anyone. It was a brutal combo. "I'm so sorry," I said to Lucas. "Okay, let's see if we can figure this out together."

We spent twenty minutes talking through flavors and numbers, and eventually settled on chocolate, vanilla, and strawberry with a few dozen "neon" thrown in just to keep with the roller skating theme. I also fell on my sword and offered to tell Mom the plan and take the brunt of her "only" wanting a few exotic flavors or only one flavor or a display that looked like a roller skate or whatever other kooky idea she had. I'd tell her this was a done deal.

Lucas and Cate were grateful, and I was glad to do it because I had a plan. I needed to tell Mom and Dad about how things had gone with Daniel, but I didn't want to talk about it in detail. Now, I would tell them we broke up and Daniel was moving before totally derailing that conversation with the cupcake news. It was a win-win for everyone involved, well, except for Mom. But then, it probably wasn't possible to give her the perfect win, so we might as well not even try.

"I do require two neon cupcakes with super-duper frosting as payment, though," I told Lucas as I walked him and Cate to the door.

"Deal," he said and casually walked out the front door to leave Cate with me in private for a moment.

"You okay?" she asked as she twisted a couple of my curls around her index finger. "It's been a long weekend for you."

I sighed. "I am. I'm sad, but at peace, which is probably just the right way to feel. I have a long hot bath and a good book waiting for me at home."

Cate hugged me and then said, "What book?"

"This mystery about standard poodles. Totally fun." Laurien Berenson's books were always a great read, and this one was no different. I needed to let myself hide in a story that was fast-paced and frivolous just now.

"Sounds perfect." Cate opened the door as she said, "You'll call me if you get lonely, though, right?"

I nodded, and I meant it. Mart and Symeon were going out tonight, and I'd assured her I was fine to be alone. I was pretty sure that was true, but I also knew how grief and loss can sneak up on you. So I really appreciated Cate's reminder.

It turned out, though, that I was just fine. I ate a frozen pizza for dinner and shared my crusts with the dogs, opened a can of tuna for Aslan only to have her pretend to be above that until I left the room, and then I got into the tub with bubbles up to my chin and finished my book with a glass of white wine.

By the time I climbed out, I was pruny and thoroughly relaxed, so I double-checked that the doors were locked, the lights out, and the animals watered. Then, I slipped under the covers and picked up *Glittering Images* by Susan Howatch. Marcus had raved about the series, so I'd snatched up the first one and was ready to tuck in. It was so good that I didn't get to sleep until eleven thirty, but the loss of sleep was so worth it.

FORTUNATELY, my Basset alarm went off just before seven, or I might have just kept on sleeping . . . or reading. That book was so good. But two dogs needed to go out, and one cat needed to tell me that she had deigned to eat my tuna but had hated it. It's amazing what a tail can express.

I put on the coffee and dropped two pieces of bread into the toaster before I picked up my phone. I had tried for a few months to not look at my phone first thing in the morning, committing instead to read in those in-between moments. But I found I couldn't really concentrate until I'd scanned my email to be sure there wasn't anything pressing.

It was a good thing I scanned while the bread toasted because Tuck needed to see me before I opened the shop. I wondered why he hadn't texted, but then maybe he didn't want to disturb me. Like most single women I knew, I slept with my phone by my bed at night, and while I sometimes slept through the vibration of texts, sometimes I didn't. Tuck knew that I had notifications turned off for email, though, so he probably knew I'd get his request in plenty of time that way. But I needed to be sure he knew he could always text me about a case, even in the middle of the night.

I blushed. "A case," I even thought of it like that, even though it wasn't mine. Still, despite my best efforts, people kept bringing me back in. I wondered if I should just succumb to the temptation and read some books on law enforcement and private investigation work. I made a note in my phone to look up some titles when I got to work.

But first, I needed to eat, shower, and get on the road. I took the fastest shower that shampoo day allowed. My thick curls required a lot of soap and even more conditioner and then leave-in conditioner and then a quick finger wave to keep them tamed in their asymmetrical cut that bobbed just below my right eye. I took a little time to spin my blue streak to the front and then pulled on my Monday clothes.

Mondays at the bookstore were pull days, the days we reviewed our inventory, figured out what hadn't sold and wasn't likely to, and then pulled the books to return to the publisher. I hated this job because I wanted to give every book and every author a chance, but it was a necessary task for fiscal responsibility. I always dressed casually on pull days because it was hard work if we had a lot of books to pull and because, subconsciously, I wanted the books we were sending back to feel comfortable with me, to trust me.

I leashed up the dogs and pondered this tendency to anthropomorphize everything while we walked to town. I'd done this my whole life. I'd said good night to every one of my stuffed animals every night when I was a child and had a steady rotation of who got to sleep in my bed so that no one's feelings got hurt. I talked to my plants about how great it was that they were going to get to fan out in the other direction now that I'd turned them around at the window and apologized to the leaves now at the back.

And the books. I told them I loved them. I thanked them for educating me. I wished them well on their return trip. To be sure, I wasn't talking to some version of the author that I connected to the books. No, it was the books themselves. When they came in with a cover that was creased, I told them I was sorry they had already been scarred by life, and when someone put a cup of coffee on an open page and left a ring, I set them near a copy of *The Velveteen Rabbit* so they could be reminded that being loved required some scars.

The funny thing was that I wasn't embarrassed by this tendency. I was, however, curious why I had it, especially when I'd been raised by two parents who were profoundly loving but

anything but sentimental. As I passed the shop and walked on
to the police station, I wondered if I might have stumbled on to
the explanation. Maybe my parents were a little too practical
for my tender heart, and these practices of mine were about
being sure the things I loved – and the people I loved – knew
they were seen and appreciated.

I was jarred out of my warm and fuzzy considerations by
the sharp efficiency of the police station. It was a small force –
just Tuck, two deputies, and the dispatcher – but this morning
they were moving with the level of focus and energy that I saw
in those police TV shows. I half expected Tuck to bang open his
office door while demanding to see the file on the Bordo case.
Instead, the dispatcher, Maude, just directed me toward his
office. "They're waiting for you," she said with a smile.

I knocked and was told to come in, and when I entered, I
noticed a spread of photos on Tuck's desk. At first glance, they
looked like something from a horror film – all these body parts
jumbled together. But then, I noticed the metal in some of the
images, the wiring in others. "Are those all prosthetics?"

Effie, across the table, nodded. "Someone in Andover, Mass
bought the contents of a storage locker at auction, and inside,
she found these." She gestured toward the photos.

I remembered this great novel I'd read called *Self Storage*,
about a young woman who buys the contents of a storage unit
and begins an intense journey propelled by a box she finds
there. "Wow. Did the winner call the police or something?"

"Right away. She was completely freaked out. Thought it
was some strange sex thing, actually," Effie was grinning as she
spoke. "We assured her it wasn't, paid the twenty-eight dollars
she'd bid to win the unit, and collected our evidence."

Tuck tapped a picture with his finger. "The serial numbers
on some of these devices, Effie said, match the devices of the
people who are missing."

I looked at the FBI agent. "Was Lizzie's arm in there?"

"It was. In great condition despite having just been tossed into a cardboard box." She frowned down at the pictures. "It just doesn't make sense. There must be several hundred thousand dollars' worth of hardware in there. Why would someone steal it and then just let the rental fee lapse?"

Tuck shook his head. "Such a waste." He sat back in his chair. "At least now you can return the devices to their rightful owners."

Something turned over in my stomach. "Will you give Lizzie's mother her arm?"

Effie studied my face for a minute. "That would be standard, but why do you ask?"

I looked down at the floor for a minute, trying to put words to the sinking feeling I had at that idea. "I don't know. Just feels off somehow. Wrong." I shrugged. "Maybe I'm just feeling defensive because of the way Mrs. Leicht talked about Lizzie's disability."

"She's pretty callous, that's for sure. I figured it was because she was to blame for Lizzie's limb loss." Effie leaned forward to study the photos again.

"Wait, Mrs. Leicht caused Lizzie to lose her arm?" I just now realized that I didn't know the story of Lizzie's amputation, and part of me felt appalled that I hadn't thought to ask that in light of Lizzie's murder but another small part, the part that was being shaped by all the reading I'd done about ableism was a little proud because I hadn't chosen to see Lizzie as her disability even enough to wonder about the story. Now, though, now I needed to know.

Effie glanced up at me. "Technically yes, but it was a car accident. Her fault but really something that would have resulted in bumps and bruises on most days." She sat back and crossed her arms over her chest. "But that day, a cement truck was coming through the intersection just after Mrs. Leicht clipped another car after running a red light. The truck creamed Lizzie's side of the car, and she had to be extracted by the jaws of life and without her arm."

I let out a hard breath. "Man. Poor Lizzie."

"And poor Mrs. Leicht," Tuck added. "Can you imagine if you had been driving and something like that happened to Mart or Cate?"

I shook my head. "No, and they aren't even my daughters. How awful." For just a minute, I let myself think about what I would feel if one poor choice on my part resulted in a significant, life-altering accident for someone I loved. Maybe I would be like Mrs. Leicht and just want to be able to pretend it hadn't happened. It made more sense, now, why she was so adamant about finding Lizzie's arm. I still didn't agree with the idea that Lizzie needed it to be whole or complete, but I could get, more, why Mrs. Leicht had such an attachment to that device.

Tuck spoke, and I pulled myself back to the conversation at hand. "Who owned the storage locker?"

"A woman named Elizabeth Chabliss. We're looking into her, seeing where that leads us." Effie sat back and began to read a file.

I studied the folder her file was in. "Elizabeth Chabliss" was written on sharpie on the tab, and the name caught my attention. I grabbed a pen and notebook from the end of the table and wrote out the name. Then, I wrote Liz, Lizzie . . . and Chablis. Lizzie Chablis. That couldn't be a coincidence, right?

Sliding my notebook over toward Tuck, I said, "I may be wrong, but . . ."

Tuck took one look at my notes and then smacked the table hard. "Doggone it, Harvey. How could we have missed that?"

He pushed the notebook in front of Effie, and she let her mouth drop open. "Lizzie rented that locker."

I raised my eyebrows and produced a fake smile. "Maybe?" I said through my teeth.

Effie took out her phone and made a call asking the person

on the other end to look into Cassandra Leicht as the potential owner of the storage unit, and then she added, "And do a search for any names related to this case that are related to the name Elizabeth and wine." She explained Lizzie Bordo and Elizabeth Chabliss and then hung up.

Effie put her arms on the table and dropped her head into them for a few moments before she looked up at Tuck and said, "Our victim stole all these devices. This case makes less and less sense the more I know."

Tuck leaned his chair back into what I now recognized his thinking position and put his hands on top of his head. "I've been tossing an idea around in my head. I'm not sure how much I believe it, but what if these devices weren't stolen?"

Effie sat up straighter. "What do you mean? How would Lizzie get all these expensive medical aids without stealing them?"

With a flash, I realized where Tuck was going with this. "You think people gave them to her, don't you?" I sat back and let that idea sink in.

Tuck nodded. "Maybe. Here's what I'm wondering. Lizzie had an expensive, prosthetic arm, but she didn't wear it when she came for her interview with Max or on the day she started her job. But there's no evidence her arm was stolen – not from here or from her apartment in Boston."

Effie slowly started to nod.

"So what if she didn't really want the arm, what if she put it in storage because she didn't want to destroy it but didn't want to live with it either?"

"Then, she met other people who felt the same way, who found their devices didn't improve their lives in the ways they had hoped," Effie added.

"Or maybe they decided they liked the way their lives were before they got the devices, that the devices weren't improvements at all." I was remembering a movie I'd seen, with Val

Kilmer maybe, where a man gets his vision restored but finds he no longer wants it, that he preferred the way he experienced the world when he couldn't see.

Tuck sat forward and let the front legs of his chair drop to the floor with a thud. "And what if someone really didn't like that? What if someone was really threatened by the idea that some people in the disability community didn't want or need devices?"

I stood up. "That's why Lizzie was killed? Is that what you're saying, Tuck?"

Tuck raised both hands. "I'm just hypothesizing, Harvey. Don't get too excited."

I took a deep breath and sat back down, and then I realized something. "Why did you want me to come in, Tuck?" I felt heat rise to my cheeks as I saw that I'd just plopped down with two law enforcement professionals and acted like I belonged.

"Actually, you've been a great help already," Effie said, "but Tuck tells me that people share things with you, that they trust you."

I wanted to be proud of that fact, but the compliment got lost in my anxiousness about what they were going to ask me to do. I sighed. "What do you need me to do?"

12

When I had imagined what Effie and Tuck were going to ask of me, I had not foreseen the words, "We need you to host a wake" coming out of their mouths. But that is exactly what they'd asked. That shock was followed by a secondary surprise when they suggested it be the next day, as in the day before a major fundraiser, as in new release day at my book store.

So of course, I said yes. Of course I did, because I'm ridiculous about wanting to be helpful.

That's what Mart said when I texted her to let her know: "Of course you did." I could almost hear the sigh through the three little dots sitting on my screen as I waited to see if she could help. "Of course I will" was her second text.

The rest of my friends responded similarly, and by lunchtime, we had a plan for food, for music (albeit simply an appropriate playlist in the background), and for drinks, two cases of wine donated by Mart's bosses. Marcus had agreed that we'd need to close the store for a couple of hours, but three to five p.m. wasn't usually a high-traffic time during the winter unless you included the teenagers who came by for espresso and flirting. We figured they'd make it if they had to flirt, uncaffeinated, in the library for one day.

All that left was invitations. It was easy enough to cover the people in town by just doing what I'd already done – told my friends. But I knew we needed to be a bit more formal. So I took a deep breath and went into Max's restaurant. He and I had already corresponded about the food, and he was glad to cater the wake and provide finger foods for everyone who came. But this conversation felt better in person because, well, I didn't really want a paper trail of what I was asking.

He was sitting at his bar looking over his books. He apparently still kept them in an old-fashioned leather-bound ledger. I'm not exactly a ballerina when it comes to my movements, so I didn't think I had to worry about not being heard when I came in. Apparently, though, I was wrong because when I put my hand on Max's shoulder, he nearly knocked me out when he threw his hand back in shock.

A few months ago, an equally awkward interchange between him and I had resulted in me having a black eye and a broken ankle, so I was glad to come away from this moment with just a sore cheek. "You ever think of going into boxing? MMA?" I asked as I rubbed my cheekbone.

He immediately went behind the bar, filled a towel with ice, and handed it to me. "Seriously, I am not safe to be around. At least not for you." He smiled, but there was a hint of something sad about his eyes, a something that was mirrored in my chest.

"Next time, I'll just bring a bullhorn and announce my entrance from the door." I smiled.

"Good. You'll be out of range from there." He pointed to the barstool next to him. "Something else you want for the wake?" He tugged a notepad from under his ledger book, and I could see the list of food we'd discussed written there in a handwriting that was half-scrawl and half almost calligraphy. It was really beautiful, actually.

"Not for the food. I think we're all set there, although if you think of something more, please add it on or substitute." He was doing me a big favor, and I didn't want to put him out at all. "No, this is more on the 'backstory' side of things."

He shifted to face me more directly and said, "There's a backstory about this wake? I suppose you mean more than the one about my bartender being murdered and keeping a storage unit full of prosthetic body parts?" Tuck had clearly brought Max up to speed.

"Well, yes, actually." I had cleared it with Tuck and Effie to bring Max into the loop because I didn't know how else I was going to get Davis back here from Boston. He'd left not more than forty-eight hours ago, and already, we were hoping he'd make the drive back to town. I thought maybe Max could help. So I filled him in on the purpose of the wake and then said, "Any thoughts on how to get Davis to come back?"

"Let me be sure I understand before I brainstorm with you." He tapped his pen on his notebook as he covered his points. "We're throwing a wake because Tuck and Agent Li think we might be able to set a trap for Lizzie's killer by dangling a lie about how they're about to make an arrest in front of the crowd. Then, your job is to talk with the two prime suspects, Lizzie's mother and Davis, to see if you can get a read on how freaked out they are by that announcement. And you're doing this because it will seem less unassuming coming from you, the humble bookstore clerk."

"That about sums it up," I said with a grin.

"No, I'm not helping you with that." Max put down his pen and looked at me.

My mouth dropped open in shock. "What? Why not?"

"It's too dangerous, Harvey. It puts you right in the middle of things, and whoever did this clearly has some issues. If they think you're onto them—"

I interrupted. "You don't think I can question a suspect without them knowing what is happening."

Max raised one eyebrow. "Question a suspect? Who are you, Dr. Reid?"

My jaw dropped open. Max Davies had just made a *Criminal Minds* reference, and an astute one at that. If I was like any member of the BAU team from the show, I was definitely Reid. Bookish, awkward at protecting myself, and far, far, far too inquisitive. I grinned. "Well, then, what do you suggest?"

"We set up a way for our suspects to feel safe talking. Make it casual but personal, too. Maybe a little corner of your shop where they can sit to have private conversations. But that way, we're all here, too. There's no need for you to be alone with a potential murderer."

The whole time he had been talking, my eyes had been growing more wide. This plan was good. Very good. I was just so surprised Max had come up with it on the spot. But then, I grew suspicious. "I like this plan, but we need to be clear about something." I took a deep breath. "This is all about finding a murderer, not about . . ." I waved my hand between us. "This is a professional arrangement. We're doing this to help Tuck and Effie, nothing else."

He raised a hand with his palm facing me and said, "I swear. You and Daniel, I know it's fresh. I wouldn't step into that grief and pressure you, Harvey." His voice was tender, honest.

I felt my heart kick up its pace and took a deep breath. "Okay, then, but we still have a problem. How do we get Davis to come back for the event?"

Max propped his elbow on the bar and rested his head on his hand in a pose very much Rodin's Thinker. For a split second, I thought about taking a trip around the world with Max to see all the presentations of that sculpture, but I quickly forced that idea from my mind and focused on our immediate problem. "I mean, it has to be good for him to make that trip back."

"It has to be good, yes," Max nodded, "but does it have to be elaborate? Maybe I can just send a text, tell him I'm worried, and ask that he come back for the wake tomorrow. Suggest I need his read on something about Lizzie's death."

I smirked. "It's so subtle and devious, and I think it just might work."

Max raised his hand into the air, and with surprise, I gave him a high five. "The tricky one, I think, is going to be Mrs. Leicht," he says.

My small jubilation of a few seconds before fades. "Oh? I was thinking she'd be easy."

"In some sense, I think you're right. It's easier for her to come, certainly, since she's in town. But does she care enough? It felt to me like a lot of the emotion at the services on Saturday was a performance."

I sighed. "You're right. I thought that, too. But in the conversations I've had with her one on one . . . I don't know. There's something under the surface. Something sad." I thought about what Effie had said about how Lizzie lost her arm, and then shared the story with Max.

"Wow. So she's exponentially grieving," Max said.

"Exponentially grieving?" I asked.

Max looked at his hands. "It's something a counselor told me once . . . that every grief after the first one is multiplied exponentially because we don't grieve each loss fresh. They build, multiply each other." His voice was very quiet, and he didn't look up.

I let that idea sit a minute, felt the accuracy of it in myself, saw it written in Max's face, and knew there was far more to this man than I'd imagined. More than I'd tried to see. The lump in my throat finally loosened, and I said, "Maybe that's what we offer her – a chance to grieve with people who can handle it?"

Max met my eyes. "You mean suggest that we're holding this event for her?"

I nodded. "And mean it. I wouldn't do that if I wasn't intent on making that so. We can set up the store in such a way that there are conversation spaces, just like you said, and then we can ask our friends to talk with Mrs. Leicht about Lizzie, give her a chance to be real about how she feels." I winced a little. "Is that too corny?"

"No, Harvey. No. That's beautiful." He patted my hand once and then twice before lifting his hand back to his hair and sliding the long sweep of blonde growing gray away from his forehead. "And I think it might work."

"But how does Davis fit in?" I felt a rush of frustration.

"I don't think Davis is a man who needs much coaxing in terms of sharing his feelings, do you?" Max raised a wry eyebrow.

I smiled. He was right. It would be easy to get Davis to talk once he was here. I put my hand on Max's shoulder as I stood. As I turned to go, I gave it a quick squeeze.

I left Max's restaurant feeling warmer somehow, heavier, too. Clearly, I had much to consider with that man, but for now, I needed to make a phone call. "Hello, Mrs. Leicht?"

THAT NIGHT, Stephen and Walter came over for dinner. Walter was famous for his five-alarm chili, and on a cold night, it was just the thing to serve with a platter of corn bread dripping with butter. Fortunately, I was masterful with a Jiffy mix, and so we had an easy meal on a night when I really needed it to be easy.

Mart poured us all glasses of Shiraz as I ladled out Walter's chili, and the four of us settled in at the dining room table while Mayhem and Taco snoozed at our feet. It would have been a perfect evening if I hadn't been so nervous about the next day . . . and the next day after that. Between the wake and the fundraiser, I expected I'd be practically sleepwalking coming Thursday.

Fortunately, my friends responded to my concern with their usual enthusiasm, and by the time dinner was over, Walter had offered to lead a brief program and invite guests to share at the wake, and Stephen had said he'd like to be the first to speak with Mrs. Leicht, if that was alright with me. "I think it might help her to talk with someone who she hasn't talked with before, let her say whatever she wants to say without feeling like she's boring people by repeating herself."

"Oh, I think that's lovely," Mart added. "When my mom died, I just needed to talk about her again and again, repeat the same stories, review the last days of her life. Each time, I felt my grief ease a little. I expect Mrs. Leicht will appreciate that, too."

I hadn't experienced death in the way my friends had, Walter had lost a brother and Stephen a partner years previous, but I knew what it was to live with loss – a marriage, a sense of calling – and I was very grateful that my friends didn't feel the need to compare suffering but simply honored pain and grief when they saw it.

Soon, the dinner table conversation turned to lighter subjects – the upcoming winter carnival that the town council had modeled after what Stephen assumed was some Hallmark movie because they'd decided the center of the small traffic circle in town should be turned into an ice rink by keeping a hose on all night so that the kids could skate the next day.

"They aren't even going to build a frame to keep the water in," Walter added with scorn. He'd owned a construction company so he knew that of which he scoffed. "I even offered to build the frame myself, but they didn't want to wait three days so I could do so."

My friends continued to talk and laugh about the skating that was going to occur by cars and pedestrians alike all around the square, but I soon lost track of the conversation as I sank into my own thoughts.

I kept circling around the idea that someone wanted Lizzie dead because, at least it seemed now, she hadn't wanted to accept their ideas of what it meant to live a good life. From all accounts, Lizzie seemed to live a great life, seemed to enjoy her days. But apparently, that wasn't enough for someone.

I pondered what it would be like if I lost a limb or woke up to find I couldn't see. The loss would be devastating, and I would probably do everything I could to recover what I had lost. But if it wasn't recoverable, would I want to replace what I had with something good but not the same? I wasn't sure. If my vision disappeared, I probably would take any chance I could to be able to read again. But then, that was the thing, right? It would be my choice to make. Not someone else's.

"Harvey?!" Mart's voice was a little sharp with worry. "Are you okay?"

I tugged myself back into the conversation and realized that I must have been zoned out in my own mind for a while. "Sorry. I was just thinking. If I lost my vision and decided I didn't want prosthetics or surgery to try to correct it, what would you guys say?" I realized that this question was probably a total non sequitur, but I didn't care.

Mart sat back and stared at me. "No vision at all. You wouldn't be able to read or see at all?"

"Right. No vision. What would you say if I decided to reconcile myself to that situation?"

"I'd say alright," Mart said, "but only after I was sure you had really thought it through and considered the options."

I nodded then looked at Stephen and Walter. "Same here," they said after exchanging a glance. "It's your life, Harvey. You get to live it the way you want."

"And if I thought I wanted to try, say, prosthetic corneas but then found I hated them, what then?"

Walter smiled. "Same, Harvey. Still your life." Then he leaned forward and grabbed my hands. "You're okay, right? This is just a thought exercise?"

"Yep, totally fine. I'm only thinking something through. I looked at Stephen and saw he had gone serious. "And what are you thinking, sir?" I asked as I tapped his foot under the table.

"It's not the same, I know," he said, "but that kind of question reminds me of the people I used to know who thought I should want to "fix" myself so that I wasn't gay anymore. I'm not broken. Far from it. I love being gay – are there hard things about it? Of course, but this is who I am, and I love my life."

"I love your life, too," I said, "and you probably don't need to hear this but just in case, there's nothing broken about you." I looked at Walter. "Either of you. You are perfect."

The men smiled at me, and Stephen squeezed my hand. "I know that, but well, it's always nice to hear it. Thank you, Harvey." He sat back and studied me. "You see what I mean, right?"

"I do, and I think that's how Lizzie felt. She had this disability. She thought she might want to try a prosthetic, found she didn't like it, and decided she was great the way she was." I felt the rightness of what I was saying as I said it.

"But someone didn't think so." Mart's voice was tight, angry. "That's what you're thinking?"

I nodded. "I do. I think someone was threatened by Lizzie's decision to discard her prosthetic. And maybe they were amped up by how she helped other people who made the same choice."

"Someone angry enough to kill might just show that anger and send a woman into hiding," Stephen added.

I sighed. "Yep, and if we're right, tomorrow is going to be

another chance for that person to reveal their rage." I just hoped we saw their anger before someone else got hurt.

I SLEPT FITFULLY, and when I woke on Tuesday morning, I didn't feel the usual joy I do on new book day. A softball-sized lump of dread was sitting in my belly, and it took all the energy I had to pull myself out of bed. Luckily, Aslan helped by kneading her needle-like claws through my quilt and into the flesh of my ankle. Nothing like pain to start the day.

Once, I was up, though, my anxious energy had me moving so fast I forgot to put sugar in my coffee and had to endure the bitter taste of the mainstream stuff we kept at home until I got to the store. Once again, my pets saved me, though, because about halfway through our walk to town, Mayhem and Taco each spotted pigeons and tried to go in different directions with great vigor. So much vigor, in fact, that they caused me to stumble and drop my coffee. I looked forlornly at the caffeine as it soaked into the lawn of a cute Craftsman cottage and then reined in the pups for the last few blocks of our walk. Now, I had no excuse but to have two lattes.

When I got to the store, Marcus was already on hand, despite the fact that it wasn't even nine a.m. I'd gone in early to prepare for the day, but I hadn't asked him to do the same. Still, I was thrilled to see him, especially today. "Bless you," I said as I unwound my scarf.

"Big day. Figured you could use the help opening up and getting things ready for this afternoon." He had already set up a table near the front windows where we could put the food for the wake. "I'm putting up the table so we don't have to do it later, but for now, I'm going to use it as a bonus releases display. Okay with you?"

I grinned. "Perfect. I don't know how many people will come this afternoon, and I don't know when they'll arrive. I have a feeling it'll be mostly local folks, but you never know. Definitely best to get as many things done now as we can, but yeah, I don't want empty tables either."

He gave me a quick salute and then threw a light blue table-cloth over the plastic table and created a lovely display that featured Ellen Hopkins's much-anticipated *Sanctuary Highway*. I always marveled at Marcus's displays with their various levels and casual symmetry. I could keep books neat and tidy, but visual creativity had never been my strong suit. Add that to the ever-expanding list of reasons Marcus was amazing.

With the opening chores done, the new releases clearly stocked both on our usual table and Marcus's new display, and my latte retrieved from Rocky's talented hands, I felt my anxiety about the day start to creep in – and at exactly the wrong time. The store was opening, and I could see a few people waiting outside. I took a deep breath, flipped on the neon, and unlocked the door.

I said good morning to each customer and did my best to look enthused to see them, and I was – at one level – but at my core, I really just wanted to be home, on the couch, with a blanket, a mug of hot cider, and a book. I could feel the tightness in my chest that warned me I was close to being overwhelmed and needed to focus on doing something that relaxed me. Unfortunately, relaxing and managing a business are not usually the best companions, but I decided to take a few minutes and slip into the backroom for a quick yoga series. Sometimes, all I needed was to focus on my breath, stretch my body, and let my thoughts skip by like pebbles across a pond.

Marcus was steadfastly handling the customers, and so I made my way to the backroom, where I'd stashed an extra yoga mat when the holiday season had gone sideways for a couple of weeks. I realized then – just like now – that if I was going to make it, I had to spend some time taking care of myself, even on the busy days. Yoga classes were out of the question because of my schedule, but I'd had enough of them in the past that with a YouTube video playing in my wireless earbuds through my phone, I was able to get fifteen minutes of a morning yoga routine in.

When I was done, I slipped my earbuds out and into their case, rolled up my mat, and took a long swig from the really cute new water bottle I'd picked up. It said, "Book Lover" on it, and the books were stacked in the shape of a heart. Mart had gotten it for me for Christmas, and I adored it . . . even if I neglected it in favor of coffee-based beverages far too often.

I was just stashing my mat in the back when I heard the click of the breakroom door as it closed. I spun around, expecting to see Marcus ready to ask me a question. Instead, I almost bumped into Mrs. Leicht. She was standing with her hands folded at her waist, and I couldn't read her expression. She looked exhausted. Her skin had a sort of green-gray hue to it, and her shoulders were hunched forward. But there was something in her expression, a steely edge that made me think she was upset, very upset. She was between me and the only way out.

I took another deep breath and willed my fear to the purposeful place of determining how I was going to get to that door if I needed to. Then, I said, "Mrs. Leicht, good to see you. Let's go out on the floor to talk. We really only allow employees in our breakroom." I stepped forward to gently take her upper arm and spin her back toward the door, but she slid away from me without moving out from in front of the door.

"I wanted to thank you, Harvey." Her voice was quiet, soft, like she was afraid to speak too loudly.

I thought about the way I always overcompensated by speaking far too softly when I'd been at a loud concert or near heavy machinery. "Thank me for what?" I was hoping she was going say the wake later today, but something about her expression didn't make me think this was gratitude for cordiality.

"For finding out why someone killed my daughter." She spread her feet wide as she studied her hands in front of her, and I got the impression of a soccer goalie ready to cover all the corners.

My heartrate kicked up, and I took a deep breath to slow it down as I wondered if I could make it under the table in the corner and out the door before she grabbed me. She was a little plump and a decade older than me, but I thought she could take me. Rage makes a woman powerful I decided against an escape attempt.

"Well, I didn't really do that." I caught myself before I revealed what I thought was the motive and felt my heart race ahead again after my near slip. "I still don't know why someone killed Liz- Cassandra?" I knew it was risky to ask a question at this point, but I literally couldn't help myself. "Why do you think I know why someone killed her?"

She took a step toward me. "Because you're smart. And I think you're compassionate, too. Those two traits, well, Cassandra had them, too, and she always understood why someone did something." Tears welled up in her eyes. "You're a lot like her you know."

My fear slid back a notch, and I let out a long sigh. "Thank you for that compliment. I think I would have really liked her."

That word of kindness broke something open. Her face crumpled, and she sank down to her knees as the sobs shook her shoulders.

13

I stepped behind Mrs. Leicht, still aware that I needed to be savvy about my safety, and then put my arm around her. "I'm so sorry," I said.

She leaned into me, and I held her up as the grief washed through her in waves. When she quieted a few moments later, I helped her to one of the chairs in the breakroom and then sat down beside her, wishing I had a cup of chamomile tea.

As if on cue, Rocky slipped through the door and set two mugs of steaming tea in front of us. "Enjoy," she said, and as she passed me, she dropped a piece of paper in my lap. I covered it with my hand and then turned back to Mrs. Leicht.

"I can't imagine what you're going through," I said. I really, really wanted to know why she thought I knew about the reason Lizzie was killed, but this woman needed my support far more than my interrogation.

"You hear people say it's the worst thing in the world to lose a child, but until . . ." she stopped and took a shuddering breath before looking at me. "She really was wonderful. And I'm not the only one who thought so. Everyone said it. She was strong and smart, but people loved her most because she listened so well."

I patted her arm as she took a sip of tea. "That's what Max said about her as a bartender. That the patrons loved her because she really listened to them."

Mrs. Leicht nodded. "She'd always been that way, even when she was a little girl. I'd take her over to a friend's house to play, and when I'd come back, the parents would say how nice Lizzie had been to their child, that she'd been so quiet but so there."

"That's a real gift, to be able to help people feel heard." I had friends who always made me feel that way, but other people in my life who should have done that for me, didn't . . . so I never took that gift for granted anymore. "You must miss her."

Mrs. Leicht's face tightened. "I've missed her for a long time, I'm afraid. I was stupid and didn't listen well myself. I pushed her away." Tears pooled in her eyes, but she didn't cave in again. Instead, she met my eyes and said, "I need to make that right."

Of course, I had a sense of what she was talking about given what people had said about how she felt about Lizzie and her decision not to use her prosthetic arm, but even though Mrs. Leicht probably knew that had come up – how could it not in a murder investigation – I decided I'd try to follow Lizzie's lead and listen. "What do you mean?"

Then, this grieving mother told me about their car accident, about Lizzie's amputation, about how the assumption had been made by herself and Lizzie's doctors that Lizzie would want a prosthetic. "I just didn't listen. She didn't want it. She hated it, in fact."

There was a plea in Mrs. Leicht's eyes. "It's so hard to understand when someone wants something different than what you'd want or what you want for them. You loved her. You did the best you could. I'm sure she knew that."

"I hope so." She sighed. "I said some awful things, though,

things I can't take back. Things I can't even apologize for now." Tears flowed down her cheeks again.

There was nothing to say to that. "I know. Someone stole that chance from you." I was going out on a really shaky limb here, but I had to push this conversation forward.

Mrs. Leicht gritted her teeth. "They did. And I want them to pay, Harvey. I want them to pay." She looked at me with a plea.

"They will. Tuck is very good at his job. He will catch whoever did this." Fortunately, I thought ahead and didn't reveal Effie's job with the FBI. "You'll see justice served." I felt confident about that, and I hoped I wasn't overconfident. Or totally misguided about Mrs. Leicht.

She stood, pushing herself up from the table, and turned to me. "I really just came here to thank you for holding the wake today. It's very thoughtful."

I reached over and gave her a quick hug, and when I pulled back, she was flushed and looked startled. "Sorry, I'm a hugger," I said.

"Listen," I moved us to the breakroom door. "I know nothing will take away your pain, but tomorrow, we're having that fundraiser for the National Disability Rights Network. I'd be honored if you'd come as my guest. It's quietly in Cassandra's honor, and I'd love to see you there."

She nodded. "I'd like that. Maybe it's a chance for me to do some things that would have helped my daughter, things she would have actually wanted."

I smiled, and we walked out onto the main floor. I caught Marcus's eye as he stood not too far away with his cellphone in his hands. He nodded, slipped the phone into his pocket, and went to the register.

"See you this afternoon, Mrs. Leicht," I said at the front door.

"Helen, please call me Helen." She gave me a wan smile and went out the door.

I headed back to the register and kept myself busy straightening bags while Marcus finished the customer's purchase. As soon as the customer left, though, I stood up and said, "Okay, how did you know about the tea? And what were you doing near the door?"

Marcus blushed and said, "I forgot to tell you this morning. I wasn't planning to use them until I did, but then, I got worried. You don't have the best track record with keeping yourself safe when talking to suspects, so I went ahead and turned them on."

I looked at him out of the corner of my eye, trying to seem skeptical, but I knew that whatever Marcus had done was smart . . . and he wasn't wrong about how I had a tendency to put myself in danger. "What did you do? Bug the backroom?"

The red in his cheeks deepened. "Not exactly. I put in a camera." He turned his phone so I could see the screen and there, clear as day, was our breakroom. "It's a really good picture, huh?"

I nodded and then stared at him. "Is this legal? I mean, I thought it was illegal to film people."

"I checked with Tuck. It's all totally fine. It's illegal to record someone's voice but not to film them. And just to cover the bases, I put some stickers in the windows to let people know." He pointed toward the front of the store.

I walked to the front, and there, sure enough, in the bottom of the two display windows was a discreet but clear sticker about video cameras being in use as well as a line in braille that I presumed said the same thing. "I totally missed those when I came in."

"Um, well, I didn't get them up until after she was in the back. Sorry." He smiled and winced and said, "Is it okay?"

I smiled. "Actually, I think it's a great idea. Might help deter shoplifters, too, and given that we've been the site of some unsavory acts in the past, it's probably something we should have done a long time ago." I scanned the upper corners of the store. "I expect they're not just in the breakroom?"

"No, there are six – one in the back, one by the doors to the bathroom, one by the back door, one in the cafe and two here on the main floor." He tapped his phone's screen and turned it to me again. "See?"

Six tiny windows showed all the various sections of my small store, and I smiled. "Now, have you already scoped out the blind corners so that when we are the site of a major heist, we'll know exactly when they donned their masks and changed their appearance?"

"I purposefully left a blind spot in the thriller section because, well, that seemed fitting." Marcus grinned and then walked me over to an alcove by an overstuffed arm chair. He had me look at the camera pointed that way and then watch as he disappeared from view for just a few seconds. When he reappeared, his hood was up, and he had the front pocket of his sweatshirt filled with mass market copies of James Patterson's books.

"Perfect," I said. "We wouldn't want to ruin the thieves' fun."

As we headed back to the register, I thanked him for his smart thinking and for keeping an eye on me while I talked with Helen. "She's really just a grieving mother," I said and hoped I was right. While we'd been talking, I'd been sure, but now, with a little space to reflect, I wondered if I had been just sold a really convincing performance. Either way, we'd have a chance to read her again in just a few hours.

JUST AFTER ONE, Tuck and Effie came in, and Marcus showed them where all the cameras were located. Then, the four of us sat down in the cafe to go over the plan. We'd set up a small conversation nook in the fiction section, and Stephen was ready to start off the conversations there with Helen after Walter led the small public program. Marcus would go next, and then he'd tap our friends one by one to go talk with the grieving mother. Everyone would be instructed to pay careful attention to what she told them about Lizzie, and we had a plan to gather after the store closed to compare notes.

"We also need to keep an eye on Davis, though," Effie said. "If he shows."

"He'll show," Max said, as he pulled over a chair and joined us. I'd invited him to come over and plan since it had been his idea on how to lure Davis back.

"He told you that," Tuck said.

"He said he'd try," Max noted, "but the way he said it . . . he's coming."

Tuck nodded. "Max, then, I suggest you be our key contact with Davis. He knows you, trusts you, it seems, and it'll appear natural for you to stay with him for most of the day since you both were Lizzie's employers."

Max let out a long, slow breath. "Okay. I'll prepare some small talk about running a restaurant, see if I can flatter him by asking for his advice."

"Good plan," Effie said. "Harvey, you'll need to be overseeing things, but let's have you be Max's back up with Davis just in case."

"Okay," I said . . . but didn't look forward to more hard conversations today. Not at all.

At about one thirty, my friends started to arrive, and like the good, thoughtful people they were, they brought food. Mostly comfort food. Mart brought my favorite orange soda and tucked a couple of bottles of white wine under the register for later. Lucas and Cate brought cupcakes. Mom carried in a pound of fudge, and Dad followed behind with a tin filled with the only thing he could make, no-cook mints.

I was beginning to wonder if I'd be unconscious from a sugar crash by the time the wake began when Lu and Tuck arrived with trays full of taco makings. Then Elle came in with a cheese tray, and Woody arrived with a chopped salad that looked amazing. Henri, Bear, and Pickle brought in a spread of pickles that featured a photo of Pickle's face right in the middle, and I laughed out loud. When Stephen and Walter carried in bottles of sweet tea and lemonade, we were all set.

Everyone set up things in the breakroom, and I sent Marcus back first so that he could be sure to get enough food. The man could eat like no one I had ever seen, and the fact that he continued to be thin as a rail was not lost on or appreciated by me. Mart hung back with me and staffed the cafe while Rocky filled a plate for herself.

Then, the rest of us tucked into the food, and by the time I'd eaten tacos, salad, pickles, two mints, a piece of fudge, and a peppermint cupcake, I was still ready to crash out, if not from a drop in blood sugar then from a too-full belly. But instead, I broke my own no-caffeine after noon rule and picked up a caffeinated latte from Rocky and set everyone to work.

It was too much effort to shift the bookshelves far, but we did manage to spin a few of the smaller ones out so that we had a sort of book-filled fan around a small central area. Marcus brought out our music stand and microphone set-up, and Walter did a test while Stephen pulled together the conversation corner that was mostly but not entirely separate from the larger space. He set a bouquet of tulips – the first ones Elle had forced in her greenhouse – on a small table between the two chairs and then slid two small footstools into place before each seat. Discreetly, he also tucked a box of tissues under the table, just in case.

By then, it was two thirty, and Marcus and I had to begin to close up shop. We had posted signs on the door, and the few patrons who were still inside began to shuffle out or over to the register to make their purchases without much prompting.

Just before three, I flipped off the Open sign and stationed myself by the front door to welcome those coming for the wake and to offer a ten percent off coupon for customers who came by and found they couldn't enter. Marcus and I had talked about allowing customers to shop while the wake was going on, just to avoid this sort of situation, but we decided it was better to put off a few customers than to interrupt the wake with the sound of the register drawer slamming. None of the four people who came to the door at three seemed peeved when I told them what was happening, and they looked delighted with the coupons. I expected we'd see at least a few of them back in the afternoon, especially since Mart's boyfriend, Symeon, had offered to bake pizzas in front of Max's restaurant to give people something to do if they wanted to wait for the bookstore to open.

Max arrived promptly at three with Helen Leicht on his arm. I smiled when I saw them, and he winked at me conspiratorially as he passed me on the way to her reserved armchair in the gathering space. Once he had helped her sit and saw that Stephen had taken up his role as escort smoothly by sitting in the chair next to her, he came back to stand beside me. "I waited just inside my restaurant until I saw her park and walk up. Wanted to play the part," he whispered.

I leaned over and briefly described my conversation with her from the morning. "So I'm not sure what to believe. At the time, she felt totally remorseful, but on reflection . . ."

"I don't know how Armand Gamache does it," Max said. "How does he keep his head straight about who to suspect?"

I stared at Max briefly. "You read Louise Penny?"

Max blushed. "A woman I know really admires her, so I thought maybe I should check her out."

Now, it was my turn to blush. I was a huge Penny fan, a fact that I didn't hide but that I also didn't know Max had paid attention to. I smiled and then forced my attention back to the gathering in front of us. A small group of townspeople had come in addition to my friends, and I was grateful they'd decided to take the time. No one here actually knew Lizzie, but we all knew what it was to lose someone, some of us very well, and so people came to show their respects and to support her mother.

At five after three, I gave Walter the nod. Tuck had suggested that we delay just a bit to give Davis enough time to arrive, but if we waited any longer, it would be obvious we'd been waiting for him, which could tip him off to the purpose here.

Walter stepped to the podium and began. "This isn't the way you usually begin a eulogy, I know, but here goes. I didn't know Cassandra Leicht – or Lizzie Bordo as she went by here – at all. But I'm sad I didn't, and the fact that I didn't know her doesn't mean her life wasn't important. It was important, especially to her mother and to the people who did know and love her."

I looked over at Helen, and while she wasn't weeping the way, say, I was, I did see moisture in her eyes, and she had accepted Stephen's hand to hold when he offered it.

Walter's short speech was beautiful. It talked about how Finn, the customer who Lizzie had served at Max's restaurant, had said she was the first person in years who had actually heard what he said, a story he'd sought out just for the wake. I looked at the back of the gathering and saw Finn there, nodding his head. Walter continued by sharing the things Max had told him about Lizzie, about how expert she was at her job, about how she'd impressed him not only with her skills but her kind spirit.

Then, Walter spoke directly to Helen. "I don't know what it is to lose a child, and I'm so sorry you do. But please know that while we did not know your daughter, we loved her just the same."

I had to take a very slow, deep breath to keep from sobbing because Walter's words were so true, so sincere. He meant every word.

Walter invited everyone to stay and talk with Helen and each other and to enjoy the food and drinks in the cafe. Rocky and Mom had worked hard to lay out the food and set up a drink station so people could talk and eat as they moved around the space. Most of the people headed right over, and after they had filled plates, they sat at the cafe tables or milled through the bookshop talking in subdued voices.

Stephen had taken Helen to our established spot, and I could see them having an intense conversation, their heads very close together. Meanwhile, Walter was moving around the room and suggesting that people make their way over to offer their condolences to Lizzie's mother, and already, people were queuing up to speak to her. Henri and Bear were the first in line, and I saw Woody a couple people later. The plan was in action.

I had all but forgotten about Davis until the door above the bell tinkled, and I saw him wheel in. He was disheveled, his collar undone and his suit pants wrinkled more than anything I, the woman who didn't own an iron, had ever worn. He looked like he hadn't shaved in two days, and his hair was standing up in places. If I'd run into him on the street, I might have thought he didn't have a home.

But this was the owner of one of the most popular restaurants in Boston. He certainly had a home. Something else was going on.

I started toward the door but felt a hand on my arm pushing me back as Max walked by me to greet our late arrival. Then, beside me, Tuck said, "Let's let him move on his own for a bit once Max gives him the official greeting as planned. I want to see what he does."

I tried to look busy refilling a tray of spicey sausage balls while I watched Davis. He went first to Effie, who must have come in the back door because she hadn't been here for the wake. Then, he said hello to a few other people, including Elle, but he moved so quickly that I didn't think they'd said anything of substance. Clearly, he was casing the room waiting to see what bombshell the sheriff was going to drop. Max's ruse had worked.

Elle came to help me mix more of the sherbet punch and said, "That man is weird." She gestured with a shoulder toward Davis. "He just asked me if I'd heard the big news yet."

I turned to look at her. "Big news?"

"I wanted to say, 'What about the murder? Well yeah.' But I just told him I had no idea what he was talking about because, well, I had no idea what he was talking about." She peered at me through tiny eyes. "Do you know what he's talking about?"

I looked away and tried to seem casual. "No idea."

"Harvey Beckett, you are the most terrible liar I have ever seen." She bumped me with her hip as I moved to rearrange the napkins into a fan. "But I won't press. I expect I'll see what's happening soon enough."

I winked at her and returned to the bookstore floor. It was just before four, and Tuck stepped toward the microphone. It was time. I just wish I knew time for what.

"Thank you for coming everyone. Harvey asked me to let people know the microphone is open if anyone would like to say a few words to honor Cassandra." He looked at me, and I smiled like I had said that very thing. "Like Walter," Tuck continued, "I didn't know Cassandra, but one of the odd pleasures of the terrible job of investigating a murder is that I get to know the victims well. Everyone I've talked to, everyone I've heard talk about Cassandra, speaks of her with deep respect and admiration. She was a strong person, no doubt. In fact, she did something that I don't know if I could have done – she accepted a terribly hard change of course in her life and not only adapted but thrived."

I glanced over at Davis and saw a vein in his forehead throbbing. Helen was sitting forward in her seat as Woody kept a close eye on her from his chair next to hers. This was about to get very intense, and I was both hopeful of that and terrified of it, too.

"Recently, I learned that Cassandra decided against using her prosthetic arm because . . . well, since she can't tell us the reason, I won't speculate. But even that choice, for whatever reason, was brave given how people view those with disabilities and given that she'd gotten a prosthetic arm and changed her mind about using it. Changing our minds is often one of the most courageous things we can do."

I couldn't get a read on Helen, but Woody had scooted forward in his chair and looked ready to jump up if need be. Davis, however, was putting forth enough fury to light a fire. His face was beet red, and he was slowly inching his chair toward Tuck. I saw Max step a bit closer to the front of the space, and when I looked over, Lucas and Mart were doing the same. We were ready.

"But not only did Cassandra make a brave choice," Tuck continued," a choice that was right for her, she also helped other people make that choice." Tuck gestured toward the front door, and Max opened it. A few people walked in and stood beside Tuck. One man was using a white cane, and another woman was missing a hand. Each person had a disability that was visible and visibly not corrected. I stared in awe as I realized that Tuck had tracked down the people who had owned the prosthetics Lizzie had stored in her storage unit. "I'd like to introduce you to Cassandra's friends."

Tuck stepped away, and the man with the cane stepped

forward. "My name is Gomez, but you can call me Go. I knew Cassandra from the bar where she worked. She was the first person to hear me say that I didn't like who I became when I could see again, the first one to tell me it was okay if I wanted to stay blind. She told me that it didn't mean I was defective or broken or incomplete. It just meant I was Go." Go was beaming as he took two steps to the left and made room for the people beside him.

One by one, each person talked about how Lizzie had reminded them that they were complete, good, beloved human beings even if they chose not to remove or lessen their disabilities. Over and over, they told all of us about her compassion, about how she had affirmed them as they were, supported them if they wanted to try an artificial limb or an assistive walking device, and supported them still when they changed their mind.

I tried to listen carefully to what each of Lizzie's friends said, but I also needed to keep an eye on Davis and Helen. Woody had reached over, and I saw that Helen was squeezing the blood from his finger. But Woody seemed okay, and I knew that if need be, he could handle that situation. It was Davis I was worried about. If he had been angry before, I didn't have words for what he was now. He'd made it almost all the way to the front of the small space we'd created, and if I had wanted to, I could have reached out and touched him.

Part of me wanted to do just that, to comfort him, to let him know he wasn't alone in whatever he was feeling. But the sensible part of me that had learned the hard way not to startle a wounded creature – cat, dog, human – stayed back. As I was wondering what we were going to do if Davis made a move, the bell over the door jingled, and I looked over to see Daniel. He smiled at me and moved into the room, and I felt myself blanch. He must have come to show support, but he had no idea what was going on. I took a deep breath. I knew him well enough to know he wouldn't stand by, as we were hoping the other guests would, if something went down.

I tried to ease my way over to him, but then, Tuck stepped back to the mic and said, "Thank you all for coming. What a wonderful tribute to Cassandra. Through Cassandra's tragic murder, I have learned something crucial, or rather, I've unlearned something that I was taught quietly, as most prejudices are. I've unlearned the idea that people with disabilities are incomplete or broken. I've unlearned the idea that everyone who has a disability should try to get rid of it or minimize it. I've unlearned the really misguided concept that I get to decide anything for anyone else about how they live, including deciding what's best for them in terms of how their bodies or minds work."

While Tuck had been talking, I had been trying to get Daniel's attention, but he was politely focused on Tuck. I had just about made my way to him with the intention of warning him, when I felt an arm catch me around the waist. Then, before I understood what was happening, my feet hit the front door of the shop, and I was in the street and moving fast.

14

As we flew past Max's restaurant and dodged an oncoming pick-up, I pulled my wits together and realized I was sitting on Davis's lap. He was very strong, and I couldn't wiggle my way free, even though I could tell he was only holding me with one arm. I tried to grab his other one, the right, as he whipped it up and back again and again, propelling his wheelchair – and me – forward, but I wasn't strong or fast enough. He just threw my arm off and grabbed it with the fingers of his left hand.

Traffic was coming at us fast as the commuters who travelled into Annapolis or Baltimore for work returned home for the night. "Get on the sidewalk, Davis. We can talk about this," I said over my shoulder.

"No, we can't," he screamed in a voice that sounded like it belonged more to a lion than to a man. "You people just don't get it!"

I squeezed my eyes shut as we just missed the front bumper of neon green Prius and then pulled myself together enough to say, "We don't get what?"

His grip on me tightened. "That there is no way to live with this kind of messed up body in this society. Not if you want to do big things. You can't just settle to be who you are. You have to be more. You have to look completely capable." He was screaming, but he was also slowing down.

Up ahead, I could see a police cruiser blocking the road, and I didn't hear any traffic behind us. Tuck had gotten barricades up.

Davis came to a stop in the middle of the road. A few cars were parked along the side, and I contemplated, for a brief second, if I could pry myself free and make it between the SUV and the sedan behind it before Davis caught me again. I decided against it because I wasn't known for speed.

I was known for talking, though, and opted for that as my best option, especially since I knew that Tuck and everyone I loved was nearby, even if I couldn't see them. "What don't we get, Davis? And who is 'we?' Abled people?" I kept my voice calm and clear, but I tried to speak loudly enough that people could hear our conversation, or at least my end of it.

He gripped my waist tighter and said, "Yeah, 'abled' people. That's the hip new term, huh? You people who don't have to work so hard to get anything because your bodies and brains operate like other people expect. You have no idea." His voice was bitter, tight.

I nodded. "I definitely don't get it." Davis's grip around me loosened just a bit. "I have no idea what it would feel like to go up to a church, say, and find there was no way in because I couldn't do steps. And while I've had moments of depression in my life, I don't know what it feels like to be completely debilitated by that kind of illness. I most certainly don't understand."

Behind me, I could feel his breath slowing, whether a result of what I was saying or the fact that we weren't hurtling down the street, I couldn't say, but I took it as a good sign nonetheless. "But I want to try. At least I want to listen and learn. That's all I can do because, at least right now, I'm not disabled. Just like I'm not a person of color, and I'm not gay. Just like I'm not a man, and I'm not a Bostonian, and I'm not a restauranteur. The only way I can understand another person's experience is to listen to them talk about it." I tried to look at him over my shoulder, but I couldn't turn my head far enough.

"That's right. You can't." His voice was still harsh, but it was calmer now, less full of rage. "I bet you don't know what it's like to be overlooked, unseen."

I sighed. Oh, I knew that experience. I expect every person did in some way, but I definitely hadn't experienced what it must feel like to be ignored because people were uncomfortable with a wheelchair. "Not the way you do, no," I said, but then I decided I might as well use this conversation for more than simple empathy. After all, the man had just kidnapped me from a public gathering. No amount of understanding was going to cover up that error on his part. "Is that why you killed Cassandra?"

The arm around my waist tightened so much that I had trouble taking a deep breath, and I heard Davis's breath go ragged again. But he didn't speak.

I knew that Tuck wouldn't let this stand-off continue much longer, so I had to ask my questions now if I wanted any chance of getting answers. "Did Cassandra overlook you? Did she not see you?" This didn't feel like an unrequited love sort of situation, but maybe I'd misread Davis. I'd certainly not anticipated that he'd grab me and run like that, so it was possible. "Did she not appreciate your attention?"

Davis twisted my torso toward him, and I winced as my achy hip protested. But now I could see his face, and he was clearly confused. "What?! You think this is about Cassandra not wanting to date me. No, I never wanted to go out with a crip—" He stopped mid-word.

"With a cripple? Is that what you were going to say?" I tried to keep the anger out of my voice, but I heard it seep in.

"That's not what I meant. I wasn't interested in dating her. That's not what this," he waved his arm around the street, "is about."

I turned a bit further to face him, very aware of how awkward it is to have a heated conversation with someone while this close to them. But Davis showed no signs of letting me stand up and move away. "What is it about then? Why are you so angry?"

"Why do you think?" He slapped his hand against the wheelchair.

I stared at him for a minute, letting my brain catch up, and then I leaned back. "Cassandra could do her work without a prosthetic, but you can't. You have to have your wheelchair."

"Bingo," he said as he jabbed a finger into my arm. "She thought she was better than me because she didn't need a device to help her. She became a full-on missionary for people to give up their tech and go 'natural.'" He spun his wheelchair in a circle, and some small part of my brain made a note to look up how he'd done that with only one arm. It was kind of cool, if also scary and a little nauseating. "She didn't get it. How hard I've had to work to get where I am, even with this wheelchair to help me. No matter what, she'd be able to get up and go to work, but me, if I didn't have this thing," he spun again as I clutched at his arm, "I'd be stuck in my house all day. I didn't want that life."

"So Cassandra tried to talk you into giving up your wheelchair?" I found that odd, but I could understand Davis's anger and frustration if she had really put pressure on him to change how he'd decided to live his life. "She asked you to stop using it?"

He grew still, and his face fell. "Well, no, actually." Then, the anger flushed his cheeks again. "But I knew that's what she wanted. She wanted to take this all away from me to make some kind of point. I didn't need to be part of her cause."

I started to explain that from what I'd heard about Lizzie, I didn't think she was like that. That in fact, I thought she probably would have advocated for him to have anything he needed or wanted to live his life on his terms. But just as I opened my mouth, I found myself being hoisted out of Davis's lap as another pair of arms reached around him and pulled his arms behind his back to cuff them.

Against my ear, Lucas said, "You're good, Harvey. Just let me get you out of the street," and he did just that. I had not imagined Lucas of cupcake-baking fame to be so strong, but he lifted me like I was a small child. To say I was grateful for his rescue would be an understatement.

Once Lucas had planted me firmly on my feet, I looked back to the street to see Tuck wheeling the handcuffed Davis toward his patrol car. For a brief second, I got anxious, worried that Tuck wouldn't know how to get Davis into the back seat since Davis couldn't stand. But I needn't have worried. A deputy came right over, uncuffed Davis, and then the two men lifted Davis into the car without incident.

Tuck gave me a two-fingered wave as he climbed into the driver's seat, and I felt all the stress of the moment leave my body. Unfortunately, most of my muscle strength also fled with the stress, and I started to crumple. For the second time that day, strong arms helped me, and I looked up to see Max as he got an arm around my waist and pulled me back upright.

Only then did I remember Daniel had been there, and I tried to right myself as I looked for him in the crowd. I really, really didn't want to hurt him, and I knew that if he got the idea that Max and I were . . . well, anything, he would be hurt. I kept swiveling my head and looking until Mart came and put her arm around the other side of my waist and whispered, "He left as soon as he saw you were safe. He said to tell you he'd see you and Taco soon."

I felt myself slump against the strong bodies on either side of me and let them steer me back into the store. The crowd was mostly still there, kept inside by Walter and Stephen, who had taken up positions as guards on either side of the door.

Marcus came in just after me and said, "Harvey, seriously, woman, I'm fast, but even I can't catch wheels at that speed." He dropped his skateboard onto the ground and smiled.

"You tried to chase me down on your board?!"

"It was the best chance we had. Luckily, Tuck had anticipated that something might go down and already had cars on the street. Who knows where he would have gone with you if they hadn't blocked traffic?"

I shuddered at the thought and realized Max but not Mart was still standing beside me. I took a step away and smiled at him as I did. "Thank you. We almost had another black eye moment back there," I said.

He smiled and kissed my hand briefly before heading out the door. "I'll bring dinner over for everyone," he gestured toward the gathering of our friends by the register. "Give me an hour."

I nodded and then went in search of the nearest chair, which happened to be the one right next to where Helen Leicht was sitting. Either she hadn't moved during that whole escapade or she'd returned to known ground for comfort. "You okay?" she asked as I dropped into the seat of the wingback chair next to her.

I nodded. "I am. A little shaken, but okay." I looked over at her and started to smile, but then I saw her face. She was about to break down and was just holding it together by clenching her jaw.

"Are you?" I asked and reached over to take her hand.

The tears came as she shook her head just slightly. "That was terrifying . . ." She tried to say more but couldn't between the gasps for air that came between her sobs. "He killed Cassandra, didn't he?"

I squeezed her fingers and leaned forward. "He didn't say he did, but given that display of anger and what he did tell me, I think so. We'll know soon. Tuck will get his confession quickly if he can."

Helen swallowed hard and then leaned back against the wing of her chair. "What did he say to you?"

I kept a hold of her hand but leaned back too, and then I recounted our conversation.

"He killed her because he thought she wanted to take away his wheelchair?" Her voice was incredulous, and I couldn't blame her. It did sound ridiculous given who Cassandra was in the world.

"I think it was more that he resented her. He seemed to be projecting his own insecurities about his need for a wheelchair onto her. She didn't need or want her prosthetic arm, so she must have thought she was better than him. That kind of thing." I sighed. "He didn't make much sense, but people with that much anger pent up rarely do." For a second, I found it sad that I knew that, knew that too well in fact.

"So he wanted her to use her prosthetic because he didn't want to feel bad about using his wheelchair? That makes no sense. Cassandra didn't care if he used a wheelchair." Helen shook her head. "I tried to tell him that."

I sat back and then I remembered seeing them talking on the street. "That's what you were doing that night on the street?"

"I wondered if you saw us," she said. "Yeah, he said he wanted to meet, to talk about Cassandra. I was hesitant. I was having a hard enough time dealing on my own, but he had known her – and I wanted so badly to talk about her with someone who had."

She sat forward and put her hands on the side of her face. "But when we met, he just wanted to explain how sad he was that Cassandra was dead and ask me questions about her death." She looked up at me suddenly. "He was trying to figure out what I knew about her murder, wasn't he?"

I sighed and nodded. "Sounds like it."

Helen shook her head. "I should have figured that out."

"Why? You didn't think he was a suspect. You thought he was her friend. Besides, even if he had said something about why he did it, you probably wouldn't have understood that as motive, right?"

Lizzie's mom shook her head. "Maybe. Still..."

"Did he say anything about your daughter and her prosthetic arm?"

"He just kept talking about how he needed his wheelchair and that he wasn't ashamed to use it. He wished more disabled people would feel the same way." She let her head drop back and looked at the ceiling. "Lizzie didn't care, not about her arm, not about his wheelchair. She just wanted people to be happy." A sob stuck in Helen's throat.

I thought for a minute and remembered some of what I read. "He did seem to think Cassandra saw everyone with a disability the same way. But she didn't, of course, at least not from what her friends here said. She saw each person as being capable of choosing how they wanted to live."

Helen nodded vigorously and sat forward. "She did. That's actually what she said to me when I pressured her to use her prosthetic. 'Mom, I know that's what you'd do in my situation, but that's not what I'm going to do, okay? It's not what I want, and this is my life.'" Tears welled in Helen's eyes again. "At the time, I thought she was just being rebellious, but now I see that she was just being strong."

I squeezed her hands again and then let them go when Rocky brought us each a chamomile tea. Both of us sat back and sipped as the rest of the crowd milled around us.

·   ·   ·

ABOUT A HALF HOUR LATER, Mart came over. Tuck had just called her. Davis had confessed to killing Cassandra. "He's sorry now," Mart said as she knelt by Helen's feet. "That's not much comfort I know."

Helen sighed. "No, not much. But is it weird if I say I feel bad for him, that he couldn't have more peace with himself like Cassandra did?"

I smiled. "I don't think that's weird at all. I think that's compassionate." As Lucas and Cate helped Helen to the door and offered to be her escort to the skating event tomorrow, I sank back into my chair and wondered if I had as much peace with myself as Cassandra did. I doubted it.

Soon after Helen left, the rest of the crowd, including Cassandra's friends who had stayed to thank me for hosting the wake, left. I immediately collapsed into tears in the fiction section. Mart sat with me while the rest of our friends returned the store to its usual layout and printed signs saying that the store would be closed for the remainder of the day. For a brief minute, I considered reopening as planned, but given that the signs had been made and included a notice about how the coupons would be honored the next day and how exhausted I felt and Marcus looked, I went with the group's decision.

Max and Symeon came over with several pizzas, a big bowl of their mushroom risotto, a giant salad, and a platter of cannoli, and I found my appetite small but there and considered that a good sign. With a plate of risotto, a symbolic portion of salad, and a cannoli, I returned to my chair in the fiction section and ate alone with my thoughts.

After I surprised myself by finishing everything on my plate, I lumbered over to my friends in time to hear Stephen say that Mrs. Leicht had shared the contents of Lizzie's will with him. Apparently, she had left pretty much everything to her mom, except the contents of her storage unit. "She left those to Johns Hopkins with the specification that the prosthetics be adjusted for new users or recycled into new equipment for people who wanted it."

"Maybe I should have made that information known earlier? " Tuck said. "Maybe it would have stopped Davis . . ." His voice trailed off.

I sighed. Maybe it would have mattered if he had, but I doubted it.

Eventually, Mart came and dragged me out the front door after asking Marcus, who happily agreed, to finish closing up the shop.

Taco and Mayhem were clearly aware that it had been a long day because they didn't pull at all as we walked. I had the sense that all the commotion had been upsetting for them, too. My impression was proven right when, after dropping onto the couch with a bowl-sized mug of hot chocolate, Mayhem broke the house rule that she never violated and jumped onto the couch to put her head on my knee. I didn't even try to object.

15

The next morning came crisp and cool, and thanks to a quiet night and a melatonin tablet, I was ready to go for the day. My body still felt like someone who weighed about a million pounds, but my mind was sharp. And I found I was actually look forward to the fundraiser that night. My enthusiasm was matched when, to my delight, I found my mother at the shop when I arrived with our guest speaker, Segarra. She was looking amazing in some sort of thigh-high fur boots, a boho shirt, and jeans that were the dream of every woman with hips.

I greeted her and shot Marcus a big thank you grin when I realized he had come in early to prepare the store for this visit. Mom took Segarra to the cafe, and I took a minute to stop by the register and speak my gratitude. "Mom talked to you about this already?"

"Yep, days ago. She didn't want you to worry though, and I'm glad you didn't know, especially after yesterday." He put his hand on my arm. "You okay?"

I nodded and sighed. "I am. Excited about tonight and also ready for it to be over, you know?"

Marcus chuckled. "Sure do. You just do what you need to do for tonight. I've got the store. Plus, there's my helper."

I looked behind me to the front door and saw Tiffany, my former employee, headed our way. "Where do you need me, boss?" she asked Marcus.

He raised an eyebrow me at her choice of words, and I laughed. "Go to it, Boss," I said to Marcus. "Good to see you, Tiffany, and thanks."

Mom, Segarra, and I had a lovely conversation over lattes and cinnamon rolls. Mom told her a little bit about what had been happening here the past few days, and I sat and listened intently as Segarra articulated what I imagined Lizzie had been living out. She talked about how disabled people are, first and foremost, people. They have preferences and needs just like anyone else, just sometimes their needs require more accommodation that our society usually gives to an individual, like a wheelchair ramp or the recognition that mental illness is a reasonable use for sick leave. She talked about devices, too, how people prefer different ways of being in the world, some preferring to keep their disabilities less noticeable, some happy for people to know about them. All in all, I came away from our conversation more informed and more committed to the event for the night.

I spent the rest of the day answering phone calls about the event, fending off reporters' questions about the incidents of the night before, and blessedly recommending a few books too.

My favorite customer of the day was a little girl named Mila who came up to me and asked, from behind her father's knee, if I had any chapter books about teddy bears. Her sweetness warmed my heart, and I had to hold myself back from skipping as I led her to the children's section.

Then, I took the slim book off the shelf and handed it to her. "This guy is so famous they've even made movies about him, but," I leaned closer with this crucial secret for any reader, "the books are always better."

Mila stared at Paddington's face on the book, and then looked up and me and said, "Thank you," before turning to her dad and saying, "Let's go."

I smiled, and as she made her way right to the register, I said to her dad, "There are some rather unpleasant stereotypes about 'darkest Peru' in there, but maybe there's an opportunity there."

He returned my smile and said, "Thanks for the heads up. I'll have the globe and some YouTube videos handy." They paid and left, and I felt – as I always did when I helped the right book find the right person – like the world was a little better for my small work.

BY THE TIME evening came around, I was so glad we were closing up early for the skating party and pretty sure I wasn't even going to lace up my skates. I was looking forward to drinking some Cheerwine from a bench on the sidelines.

Marcus and I finished closing the shop and flipped off the sign, and then, Rocky broke her own rule about dogs in the car and let Taco and Mayhem lounge on her backseat with me so we could drop them off at home.

As usual, my friends and parents had done a superb job of readying the place. The decorations were awesome – total '90s with hot pink and mint green. They'd even put out a table of 90s accessories, including scrunchies and baseball caps with bling. My parents greeted me by the food table, and it took me a minute to realize they had dressed up. Dad was in khakis and his usual boat shoes, but the fanny pack around his waist – not around his shoulders as was cool here in the 21st century – pulled the whole look together. And Mom was in overalls with a T-shirt underneath and a flannel shirt tied around her waist. It was like looking at me from twenty-five years ago.

Heck, it was like looking at me now. Before we'd left the store, I'd changed into my favorite outfit – wide-legged jeans, Birkenstocks, and a vest over a snug long-sleeve T-shirt. I honestly hadn't been thinking '90s when I dressed, but well, I guess my true self was '90s. I pulled my vest out in front of me and studied it, realizing only then that I'd actually had the tan corduroy piece since college, when I got it at a local church's free clothing room. I sighed. What was I going to do with myself?

But when I saw Marcus emerge from the restroom with the full-on '90s hip-hop look, Timberlands, big chunky gold jewelry, and a bucket hat, I could not stop smiling. Oh, this was going to be fun.

I made my way to the beverage counter and grabbed my drink before scouting out the best place to sit. I wanted to be sure to be able to help as needed, but I also wanted to see the skating floor. Plus, I wanted to be pretty anonymous and just stay in the corner. I spotted a small table near the door, where I'd see if Mom's team was flagging and where I could keep an eye on the floor but mostly be out of sight.

I had just put my butt in the chair when Mart came over and dropped a pair of roller skates at my feet. I looked from the skates to my best friend and started to laugh. "Oh my word, you looked like this in college, didn't you?" I said.

She grinned. "Pulled these right out of my closet." She was wearing jeans with rips in the knee and a flannel shirt over a Pearl Jam T-shirt with Doc Martens, and her hair was in pigtails. "It's a little embarrassing."

"Tell me about it," I said, as I waved a Birkenstock-clad foot at her. "I wasn't even trying to dress up."

She cackled and said, "Lace up. You're on in five."

Out of habit, I looked at my phone to see the time – 6:55. But

I wasn't supposed to do anything tonight. That had been the agreement I'd made with Mom. I needed a night off, and she'd agreed. "I'm not a part of the program, Mart. Mom's got this." I nudged the skates away from me and sat back.

"Nope, not tonight," she said as she pulled on her skates. "You're not on tonight, so that means one thing – we let loose." She knelt down and slipped off my shoe, making me – for the first time ever – regret my love of Birkenstock clogs. Then, she slid my foot into a skate before putting on the other one. "All Skate is the first one. Let's go."

She jerked me to my feet so fast that I almost spilled my Cheerwine. I groaned, but I didn't resist too hard. I was a forty-five-year-old woman. If I fell, I fell.

And I fell. Right away, as soon as my skates hit the slick floor. That was a bit embarrassing, but I was more mortified by the fact that I couldn't get up because I was laughing so hard. Fortunately, Mart sat down next to me for company.

Then, Elle, the show-off who skated backwards, came over and pulled us to our feet. Fortunately, I got my skate-legs under me more quickly than I had as a teenager when I'd been too self-conscious to try anything until I was perfect at it. A few loops around, and I was skating away to Michael Stipe and having a blast.

After a few minutes, Mom took the microphone in the DJ booth and got everyone's attention. We all turned toward the small podium now at the edge of the rink and listened as Segarra thanked us for coming and talked about the reasons disabled people needed our advocacy. She told stories about places she couldn't enter because there were only flights of steps to get inside. She talked about people using the bigger stalls in bathrooms to change their clothes when she had to use that one if she had her walker so that she could actually, well, use the bathroom. Then, she asked us to take a challenge: every time we visited a public place, we needed to think about a disabled person we knew and try to see if they could navigate that space easily and with all the accommodations they needed. I knew then we needed to make a point of suggesting to the owners that they make some changes.

Her speech was brief but rousing, and I could see a lot of people nodding their heads around the room. I knew St. Marin's was going to be a more accessible place from now on, and I was glad to be a small part of that work. But when Segarra was done speaking, she said, "Now, let's skate!" and I couldn't wait to get moving again.

Elle, Mart, and I laughed our way around the rink a few times, and eventually, Mom and Henri joined us. Soon, we were a full-on Red Rover line of women rolling our way around the rink. Small children skated under our arms, and not a few men our age tried to break our line, sending us spinning and tumbling with laughter. I hadn't had that much fun in a long time.

But then, the lights dropped and "Hold On" by Wilson Philips came on, and I realized we were about to enter a Couples' Skate. The idea had terrified me when I was young, and I wasn't much less fearful now. I was making my way to the edge and aimed for my now watered-down soda when a hand grabbed mine and spun me around.

There I was, face to face with Max, and I was so exhausted and giddy from laughter . . . and well, from his presence, that I felt light-headed. "Skate with me," he said.

I nodded and let him pull me to the floor. We held hands like we were twelve and made our way around the ring in silence until the song ended. Then, he looked at me and said, "Thank you," before skating off to help with the DNRN information table.

Mart didn't waste any time skating over. "A Couples' Skate with Max? Well, well, well."

I smiled. I had no idea what was going on, and for once, I was okay with that.

And when "Gettin' Jiggy Wit It" came on, my girls and I headed onto the floor again to let Will Smith dance us into the night.

Harvey's next adventure, *Proof Of Death*, comes out in July. Pre-order here - https://books2read.com/proofofdeath

HARVEY AND MARCUS'S BOOK RECOMMENDATIONS

Here, you will find all the books and authors recommended in *Scripted to Slay* to add to your never-ending to-read list!

- *Babel Tower* by A. S. Byatt
- *A Bear Called Paddington* by Michael Bond
- *Being Heumann* by Judith Heumann
- *Black Magic Kitten* by Sara Gorgeous
- *Blue Highways* by William Least Heat Moon
- *Brother Odd* by Dean Koontz
- *Burning Your Boats* by Angela Carter
- *Calypso* by David Sedaris
- *Cat of the Century* by Rita Mae Brown
- *The Center Cannot Hold* by Elyn R. Saks
- *Chocolate Chip Cookie Caper* by Joanna Fluke
- *Concrete Rose* by Angie Thomas
- *Crossing to Safety* by Wallace Stegner
- *The Dirty Life* by Kristin Kimball
- *Falling for your Best Friend's Twin* by Emma St. Clair
- *The Glass Castle* by Jeannette Walls
- *Glittering Images* by Susan Howatch

- *Laughing at my Nightmare* by Shane Burcaw
- Mandala Coloring Books by Dover Press
- *A Pedigree to Die for* by Laurien Berenson
- *Remote Control* by Nnedi Okorafor
- *Sanctuary Highway* by Ellen Hopkins
- *Self Storage* by Gayle Brandeis
- *Shadow and Bone* by Leigh Bardugo
- *There There* by Tommy Orange
- *The Velveteen Rabbit* by Margery Williams
- *The Watchman of Rothenburg Dies* by Adriana Licio
- *We Free the Stars* by Hafsah Faizal
- *The Beautiful Mystery* by Louise Penny

WANT TO READ ABOUT HARVEY'S FIRST SLEUTHING EXPEDITION?

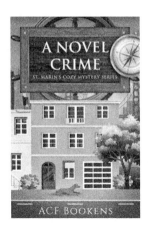

Join my Cozy Up email group for weekly book recs & a FREE copy of *A Novel Crime*, the prequel to the St. Marin's Cozy Mystery Series.
Sign-up here - https://bookens.andilit.com/CozyUp

CROSSED BY DEATH - A FREE PREVIEW OF ACF BOOKENS' NEW STITCHES IN CRIME SERIES

Crossed By Death
Chapter 1

I cinched the scarf more tightly around my head and wedged the hard hat into place. I'd learned the hard way that not covering my hair and my head could mean a mess, sometimes a bloody one.

The doorframe appeared to be solid, and when I pushed hard against the floorboards with my right foot, they held solid, too. I walked into the Scruggs Store and crouched beneath the collapsing roof. Not much left here I could safely search through, but I was going to do my best. I'd paid good money for this salvage job, and I was going to get what I could.

I'd driven past this old gas station all my life and had mourned as the vegetation took it over and began to pull it down over the past few years. I knew, though, that no one in our rural mountain county was going to buy the place, not after someone had been murdered there twenty years ago. A single gas pump on a country road wasn't enough incentive to take on that bad mojo.

It was a loss, though, because the station had been there for almost a hundred years – first as a country store and then as a welcome fueling spot twenty-five miles from the nearest city. I was determined to not let it all disappear when the bulldozers parked outside knocked it down. My fifty dollars had gained me entry and rights to anything I could carry out before the station was destroyed, and I was going to get my money's worth while saving a bit of history along the way.

I was new at the salvage business, but I knew enough about local history and had watched enough *Barnyard Builders*, *American Pickers*, and *Salvage Dawgs* to feel like I could find the good stuff. I headed to the left toward what used to be the check-out counter and hit paydirt right away. The original counter was still there, complete with a hand-written sign about check cashing as well as a Virginia lottery sticker from somewhere in the last decade of the previous century. A few coats of poly on this baby, and it would make a great piece of wall art for someone who loved that 1990s feel or just wanted to relive their heyday.

A few good pries with my crowbar and I had the whole countertop sitting by the door ready to go. That piece alone was worth my investment, but I wanted to go a bit further in, see if maybe there was some old stock of soda or something. People paid ridiculous prices for skunked beer and flat Pepsi. The coolers were underneath some rafters, so I moved gingerly toward them. Most of the shelves were empty, probably raided before the building started to cave in, but I could see the glint of light off glass in the back. Jackpot! The overstock was still there, it seemed.

I picked and tested my way to a door that seemed to open behind the wall of refrigerated units and prayed it wasn't locked. I didn't feel like kicking in a door and bringing down the roof. Luckily, the knob turned, and I was in. Not cases and cases of old stock, but enough to turn a good profit. As I carried out a few boxes of soda and Yuengling, I thought about how tight the margin for a store like this must have been. The owner had to keep enough supply to satisfy customers' last-minute shopping needs – gallons of milk, snacks, a few packs of diapers probably – but not so much that he couldn't make a profit on what he stocked. It was hard going.

Maybe it was easier, though, since he and his family lived at the back of the store, like a lot of shop owners back in the day. I thought about what it would have been like to grow up in that little house, to have people coming by all times of day and night to get cigarettes or pick up a sandwich from the little kitchen in the back of the store. I might have loved it, and I knew my son, Sawyer, would have thrived with all those people to talk to. His extroverted tendencies were in diametric opposition to my introverted ones. But I thought it probably also would have grown tiring and tedious.

As I set a sixth case of Cheerwine by the door, I made my plan for a last foray into the store and then, hopefully, into the house behind. I could just make out a doorframe in the far back corner, and since I'd noted the exterior bathroom doors before I came in, I figured this must be the way into the house. The only problem was that I was going to have to crawl my way back there. My forty-six-year-old body wasn't much for crawling despite the fact that Sawyer was in a "Be a rhino with me, Mommy" stage.

Still, that little boy needed his mommy to buy him cheese crackers and milk, so crawl I did. And when it was necessary for me to be thinner than my crawling hips would allow, I shimmied my way like a snake and decided I wasn't going to suggest Saw and I try that animal imitation out.

I made it to the door, though, and I was hoping that the quick look I'd had at the house hadn't been deceptive. Luckily for me, this roof was still standing at its full eight feet. I levered myself to standing and looked around at what reminded me of the living room of my high school years. A big black television from before the age of flat screens sat in one corner, and in front of it, a couch with overstuffed arms and red plaid fabric was under a rumpled blanket and a throw pillow. It looked like someone had just gotten up from a Sunday afternoon nap.

A quick scan told me there wasn't anything worth hauling out of here, but I was glad to find that the exterior door was easy to open in case I did find anything. If only I had seen it before I covered my entire front in dust from my army crawl back here.

I made my way into the kitchen and felt sorrow hitch in my chest. A wire rack with moldy cookies was waiting next to a plastic tub designed just for cookie storage. My mom had the same one, and I loved coming home from school and raiding the freshly baked stash. Beside it, the mixer was bowl-less, and I saw the stainless-steel bowl in the sink, ready to be washed. A mug of half-drunk tea sat at the edge of the counter. Someone, probably a woman, probably a mother, had been interrupted in her work.

I took a deep breath and said a word of gratitude to that woman before I started flinging open cabinets. I only had a few more minutes before Saw or our Maine Coon cat, Beauregard, got bored of watching funny cat videos in the car or someone saw them and came to investigate who had abandoned their toddler and a giant feline in their Subaru Outback at a derelict gas station. It wasn't my favorite choice of things to do, but Sawyer was safely in his car seat, the car was locked, and Beau was better than any guard dog, especially since he weighed in at a solid twenty pounds under his copious striped fur. The plight of a working single mom required creative problem solving, and sometimes creative problem solving involved a guard cat.

I found some vintage cookie cutters and a set of Corel dishes that I quickly loaded into the dishpan I had emptied into the sink. If I couldn't sell them, then someone would appreciate the set at Goodwill. A few pottery mugs and really nice knife block I could use at home rounded out my haul from this room.

After I deposited those items on the small porch outside the living room door, I plunged into the first of the bedrooms. I didn't think there'd be much to salvage here since the clothing wasn't going to be old enough to be truly vintage, but I hoped to maybe find some children's clothes in good shape for Sawyer and maybe a coat for me. I hit the jackpot straight off. Lots of four T pants and shirts that would fit Saw in a matter of weeks at the rate his two-year-old body was growing and even a couple of pairs of shoes. I tried not to think of the murder when I was in this room, but I prayed for this little boy. Prayed he was okay in all the ways.

There looked to be only two more doors in the small hallway, and the one at the end of the hall was likely the bathroom. I hadn't been in many abandoned houses, but I'd learned the hard way that opening the bathroom door was a bad idea. I skipped that one and went on to the other bedroom.

The curtains were pulled tight, and while the light would have been helpful, I was in a hurry. I just headed for the closet with my flashlight and rifled through the clothes before pulling boxes down in case there were antiques or any particularly great caches of photos or mementos I needed to rescue. When I had started this work, I'd made a vow that I would try to return anything personal to the owners if I could, so I always salvaged photo albums, boxes of children's art, and any other pieces of family history I could. Then, I spent ten percent of the money I earned from selling the other things to try to get those back to their owners. I couldn't afford to do more than that in terms of shipping or ads in local papers, but I figured the least I could do was try that. Sometimes, it worked. Often it didn't, and if it didn't, I tried to console myself with the fact that maybe people just wanted to leave the past behind altogether. I probably would.

I didn't find a coat for me in the closet, but I did see a small jewelry box shoved up on a high shelf. I chuckled. My jewelry box was in exactly the same place because Sawyer had developed a deep interest in wearing – and breaking – every necklace I owned. I wasn't about to let him swallow my grandmother's diamond ring, not when that was our financial back-up as well as a precious memento of my granny.

I tucked the jewelry box under my arm and turned to swing my flashlight around the room. As my light swept over the bed, I saw a lump in the corner under the window. I thought it might be a pile of discarded clothes, and with winter coming soon, I found myself praying that someone might have discarded their coat over a chair. The fact that my heart was racing made me pray even harder.

I made my way around the bed to get a closer look, and I clenched my teeth to keep from screaming. A woman was sitting in an armchair, and she wasn't moving – not even breathing.

I stepped back, took a deep breath to push down the panic because I didn't want to alarm Sawyer, and walked out of the side door of the house.

It felt awful to have to drive away from that house, but there was no cell service for a couple of miles. I threw the jewelry box in to the floor below where Beauregard reclined like the prince he was and headed north toward town. As soon as my phone showed three reliable bars, I pulled into the nearest driveway and dialed 911.

"Yes, this is Paisley Sutton. I just found a dead body in the old store on Scotch Road."

The dispatcher, used to traffic accidents and reports of four-wheelers on the roads I imagined, was a bit flustered, but he managed to tell me he was sending officers and that I should wait there. I explained I was two miles up the road and would get back to the store as soon as I could. He didn't even ask why I'd left the scene. We all knew the mountains wreaked havoc with cell service.

"What we doing, Mommy?" Sawyer asked from the back seat.

"Mommy has to talk to the police, Love Bug," I said as I ripped open a packet of fruit snacks with my teeth and handed it to him as I simultaneously swung the car back onto the road toward the store. "You're going to get to see police cars!" My son loved anything vehicular, and I was counting on flashing lights and maybe a kind officer who would show off a siren to help my toddler though this change of plans. He was going to miss his playground time, and if these police cars didn't make up for slides, it was going to be a hard fight for a nap.

My maternal worries were mostly allayed though as Saw started bouncing in his seat as soon as he saw the blue flashing lights by the store, and when I pulled over and told him to wait patiently, he said, "I will, Mama," and craned his little neck to see the police officers in uniform.

I walked to the first officer I saw and introduced myself. "I found the body," I said, and the young black woman nodded. Then, she looked over my shoulder at the car. "Your son?"

I smiled. "Yeah, I'm a single mom, so he goes with me every-where. He doesn't know what's happening, but he sure is excited about seeing police cars."

She snapped her notebook shut with such briskness that I had a flash of fear that she was going to scold me for neglect. Instead, she tilted her head at the car and said, "Mind if I sit with him?" She pointed to the radio and flashlight on her belt. "My guy loves my toys."

I felt a flood of relief as she headed toward the backseat of my car and knocked on the door before asking Sawyer if she could sit down. When she patted her knees and let Beau settle in her lap while Sawyer squawked her radio to high heaven, I knew he'd be fine and went to see what I could find out about the woman inside.

An officer was on the front stoop of the store, and so I walked up and tapped him on the shoulder. When he turned, I recognized his face from the election posters I'd seen around the county for the past couple of months. He was our new sheriff, Santiago Shifflett, the first Latino sheriff in the area, and, thankfully, the man I'd voted for.

"Sheriff, I found the body." That was a sentence I hadn't thought I'd utter even once in my life, but here I was saying it again. "Want me to take you in?"

"Ms. Sutton, thank you for calling it in. We actually found her already, but I would like to ask you a few questions." His voice was kind but serious.

"Of course." I had prepared as best I could to tell my story in the few quiet minutes of the drive back to the store. "Do you mind if we sit though? Sawyer, my son, got up at five-thirty, and the adrenaline is starting to wear off."

"Sure," he said. "That work?" He nodded toward the bulldozer at the edge of the lot and headed that way.

I climbed up in the seat, and the sheriff stood below. A deputy brought over two bottles of water, and I gulped mine down with gratitude. "What do you need to know?"

Sheriff Shifflett leaned against the tracks of the dozer, and I felt a little of my tension ease. If he wasn't worried about getting his uniform dirty, I felt like I could trust him. After all, I walked around with some stain – food, poop, playdough – on my clothes every day of my life. "Let's start with why you were in the house."

I pulled out my business card with "Save The Story," the name of my business, printed across the top. "I do historical salvage from old buildings. The owners gave me permission to go inside and take whatever I could." I gestured to the stack of soda and beer beside the small circle of officers on the store's porch.

The sheriff glanced over his shoulder and the back at me. "You found soda?" There was a lightness to his tone, and I could just see the start of a smile in the corner of his mouth.

I smiled. "I know, right? People pay a lot of money for old soda."

"They want the soda itself? Not just the bottles?"

"It's kind of like having old toys in the original box. Original condition means more value, I guess." I shrugged. "I don't question it. I just buy groceries with it."

Shifflett pursed his lips. "Whatever it takes to pay the bills." Sometimes people said that with mockery, but the sheriff seemed sincere.

"Exactly." I then told him about searching the house and about going into the back bedroom. "That's when I saw her. I didn't touch anything, and I'm sorry I had to leave the scene but—"

"Cell service, I know." He turned and looked at the house. "Did you notice anything unusual in there?"

I looked back up at the store and then beyond it to the attached house. "No. I mean, it's was disconcerting to go into that house and see that it was like the people who lived there had been abducted by aliens. But I assume they left a long time ago, like after the first murder."

The sheriff turned back to me. "You knew about that then? And you still went in?"

"Like I said, groceries." I'd grown up nearby, and the murder had been a big deal, especially because they thought it had been someone who frequented the store. "Besides, there's a story there, one that needs to be remembered, and not just the story of the murder, the first one, I mean. Those people had lives before and after the father of that family was killed. I wanted to remember that, to help other people remember that." I took a deep breath, surprised that I'd shared that much with this man I'd just met. It wasn't really relevant to the investigation, after all.

But the sheriff didn't seem put off at all when he turned back to me. "I get it. Part of why I do my job, too. Crime happens to people and is committed by people. It's not just a thing that happens or that happens in one moment and then is gone. It's the people involved that get my attention."

I studied the sheriff's face for a second and then nodded. But then, I heard Saw's call, "Mama!" and knew my time was limited. "I hate to ask, but can I take the things I gathered from the house?"

He shook his head, "I'm afraid not. They're part of the crime scene. But if you have a minute," he glanced over his head toward the car, "maybe you could show me what you were taking. It'll help us sort out the scene but also, hopefully, I can get it to you later."

I nodded. "Of course." I took a quick look at my car and saw the deputy handing Sawyer her radio and gauged I had about five more minutes. I quickly walked him through the store and pointed out the countertop and the cases on the porch before showing him my haul outside the door of the house. He made notes and studied each pile of goods.

I heard Sawyer's wail again and knew I needed to go. "Thanks, Sheriff. You have my number, so call if I can help further." I waved as I jogged around the front of the store.

I hurried back to the car, where Sawyer was working up a good tantrum. I thanked the officer, gave my son a kiss on the forehead, and then climbed into the car. Eleven fifteen – it was time for a picnic lunch before my toddler went into total meltdown.

Order *Crossed By Death* here - https:// books2read.com/crossedbydeath

ALSO BY ACF BOOKENS

St. Marin's Cozy Mystery Series

Publishable By Death

Entitled To Kill

Bound To Execute

Plotted For Murder

Tome To Tomb

Scripted To Slay

Proof Of Death

Stitches In Crime Series

Crossed By Death

Bobbins and Bodies

Hanged By A Thread

ABOUT THE AUTHOR

ACF Bookens lives in the Blue Ridge Mountains of Virginia, where the mountain tops remind her that life is a rugged beauty of a beast worthy of our attention. When she's not writing, she enjoys chasing her son around the house with the full awareness she will never catch him, cross-stitching while she binge-watches police procedurals, and reading everything she can get her hands on. Find her at bookens.andilit.com.

f facebook.com/BookensCozyMysteries

Printed in Great Britain
by Amazon

80719067R00122